Ernest McGaffey

Poems

Ernest McGaffey

Poems

ISBN/EAN: 9783337156473

Printed in Europe, USA, Canada, Australia, Japan

Cover: Foto ©Andreas Hilbeck / pixelio.de

More available books at **www.hansebooks.com**

University Press:
JOHN WILSON AND SON, CAMBRIDGE, U. S. A.

Inscribed

TO MRS. G. H. NELSON,

FROM HER AFFECTIONATE
NEPHEW.

CONTENTS.

———◆———

Songs and Lyrics.

Outdoors.

Warp and Woof.

5

Foam-Wraiths and Driftwood.

My Chapter.

6

In the Sunset Lands.

SONGS AND LYRICS.

SONGS AND LYRICS.

---◆---

AND EVEN I.

THE lark lies dead upon the plain,
    The wood-bird sits with folded wing,
Leaps in my breast the old refrain,
    Still must I sing, still must I sing.

Nay ! not because Parnassian height
    Seems nearer now or less sublime, —
High, high indeed, his muse's flight
    That soars beyond the lapse of time, —

But that my songs, when I have passed
    The shore-line of the Stygian Sea,
May be in some man's heart at last
    What other songs have been to me.

11 '

No higher hope I hold than this,
    That one may say when I am dead,
" He reckons not of death's cold kiss ;
    His song shall answer in his stead."

And thus a changeless trust I keep
    My guiding star in stormy years,
Or when I wake or when I sleep,
    That bids me through all doubts and fears

To stake my soul upon the die,
    And write some lines that will not rust, —
A great heart-hunger not to lie
    Forgotten when my bones are dust.

THE CROW'S WING.

CURVING sweep of a burnished wing
Black as the gloom of a winter night,
Strong in a sense of hardy flight
Over the woods and the mountain height,
Winds and the white moon following.

What though the lightning's fancies played
Hide and seek in the darkling skies,
Thou on the storm's broad breast didst rise,
Sailing on as an arrow flies
Loosed at a foeman's ambuscade.

What though the hail made fierce attack
Beating down on thine ebon wings,
Rain that chills and the sleet that stings, —
Naught to thee were these buffetings
Borne along in the tempest-wrack.

13

Holding still to thine airy path
Silent, stern as the seal of fate,
Thou hast learned an to watch and wait,
Morn break soon or the stars rise late,
Come what may for the aftermath.

Send my soul on a sable wing
Death, when the darkness falls on me;
Let me wander by land and sea
Free as the crow's flight, yea, as free,
Winds and the white moon following.

BROTHERS AND SISTERS.

BROTHERS I have by the score,
A million, yea, and more ;
Men who are striving 'mid sun and rain
Resolute comrades on hill and plain,
Drawers of water and hewers of wood
Bound in a common brotherhood,
With the hearts and hands to dare and do
Life's fiery furnace passing through,
Oh ! brothers, I pray for you.

And sisters have I, yea, more
Than sand-grains by the shore ;
Women who work, and who know not peace
Sighing in vain for the soul's release ;
Sisters of trouble, in poverty's van
Toil-worn faces I sadly scan,
They come and go and are lost to view
And death shall linger and fate pursue,
Oh ! sisters, I weep for you.

FLIGHT.

A HICKORY tree in the valley grew ;
  The snows and sun and the spring rains
    found it,
And shrill-voiced winds from the northward
    blew,
  And the dews in the night-time fell around it.

Deep into the earth its fibres crept
  And pierced the flint in the depths down
    under,
Till the lightning out from the cloud-ways
    leapt
  And the hickory fell, and was split asunder.

And there by its side the shadowy marsh
  A crane's nest held by the curving river,
Where the tall grass mingled, coarse and harsh,
  With reed-beds broad and the sedge a-quiver.

16

And the tree and the egg and the stone lay
    there
  But shreds and shards at the dim earth's
    portal,
As common things that could never dare
  The higher realm of the far immortal.

But an Indian wrenched from the tree a shaft
  And struck a flint from the rock-ribbed
    ledges,
And a crane's quill picked from a tangled raft
  Of reeds and weeds by the brown marsh-
    edges.

And the arrow sped from his twanging bow
  Till the lone blue vault of the sky was riven,
And that which was humblest here below,
  Now at the last was the nearest heaven.

AT THE WAYSIDE INN.

MINE host of the wayside inn,
　We seldom see him there ;
But the waiter, tall and thin,
　With his puritanic air,
He comes, and brings us wine,
　Then leaves us there alone, —
She with the vintage brought from Rhine,
　I with the juice of Rhone.

Oh, girl with the golden hair
　And eyes of iris blue,
Has Troy's own Helen fair
　Changed places, then, with you ?
.No face of woman yet
　To me so much hath been,
And I with you all else forget
　Here at the wayside inn.

18

And the cuckoo clock on high
　　Keeps up its race with time,
And still, as the moments fly
　　Drones out with mellow chime.
" Cuckoo," as the quarter falls
　　It sounds in plaintive tone ;
" Cuckoo," at the half it loudly calls
　　Then leaves us there alone.

Oh, girl with the golden hair
　　And the red rose at your breast,
You are fair, mayhap too fair,
　　But, bah ! you are like the rest,
And why should I to-night
　　These vain romances spin,
That still with the curling smoke take flight
　　Up from the wayside inn ?

And the wine in the glasses glows
　　As slow and slow we sip,
While the heart of the red, red rose
　　Has kissed at last her lip,
And the flame on the hearth-stone sinks
　　As the embers turn to gray,
And the bead on the bubbling grape-juice blinks
　　Just once and melts away.

Oh, girl with the golden hair,
 Know this before we part :
I share and do not share
 I give, yet keep my heart ;
For pride will stand all test,
 And you no word shall win
From the careless wight who loved you best
 There at the wayside inn.

VÆ VICTIS.

I SING the woe of the conquered, a winding-
    sheet for the slain,
Oblivion's gulf for those who fell, who strug-
    gled and strove in vain.

As of old, mid the plaudits of thousands, may
    the victor in triumph stand,
While the blood of the vanquished trickles
    down and reddens the yielding sand.

For the living the martial music, and the clus-
    tering laurel wreath ;
Let the dead rust on forgotten, as a sword in
    a rusty sheath.

On the face of youth and health and strength
    should the blessing of sunshine fall ;
A single shadow may well suffice the face that
    turns to the wall.

And he who has taken a mortal hurt in the
strenuous battle of life,
Let him creep away from the dust and din,
from the arduous toil and strife,

Let him go as a wounded animal goes, alone,
and with glazing eye,
To the depths of the silent fastnesses, in silence
there to die.

For the prow of the ship rides high and free
that baffles the savage gales,
And the wind and rain is a requiem for the
wreck of the ship that fails.

A DANCER.

In the lamplight's glare she stood, —
The dancer, the octoroon, —
On a space of polished wood
With glittering sand-grains strewn ;
And a rapid, rhythmic tune
From the strings of a mandolin
Leaped up through the air in viewless flight
    and passed in a strident din.

Her eyes like a fawn's were dark,
But her hair was black as night,
And a diamond's bluish spark
From its masses darted bright,
While around her figure slight
Clung a web of lace she wore,
In curving lines of unhidden grace as she
    paused on the sanded floor.

23

Then the clashing music sprang
From the frets of the mandolin,
While the shadowy arches rang
With insistent echoes thin,
And there, as the spiders spin
Dim threads in a ring complete,
A labyrinthine wheel she wove with the touch
    of her flying feet.

To the right she swayed, — to the left,
Then swung in a circle round,
Fast weaving a changing weft
To the changing music's sound,
As light as a leaf unbound
From the grasp of its parent tree,
That falls and dips with the thistledown afloat
    on a windy sea.

And wilder the music spell
Swept on in jarring sound, —
Advanced and rose and fell,
By gathering echoes crowned ;
And the lights whirled round and round
O'er the woman dancing there,
With her Circe grace and passionate face and
    a diamond in her hair.

A SONG OF DEATH.

As a bird to its nest, a man to his home, a
    child to its mother,
    I, who have tossed on the sea of life as a
      leaf on a wind-swept heath,
Turn from the hearts of those I love, — from
    sister, father, and brother, —
    Turn with a smile on my lips and come, to
      meet and greet thee, Death.

Thou art the key to the vast unknown; with
    thee are the dark abysses
    That stretch between grasses and stars, and
      divide us from those we love.
Welcome art thou to the broken-hearted, —
    thine icy kisses
    Are a message of hope, as in olden days was
      the olive branch borne by the dove.

As the germ to the sprout, to the tree and the
leaf, so change is common
And the dead leaf lives in the spring-time
grass, and nothing really dies.
Shall blades of grass be immortal, and never a
man or woman?
We are all a part of nature still, and nature
never lies.

Hail, silence, and open the prison doors that
herald the soul's release!
Farewell? 'T is a beautiful word, to be
uttered with even breath.
Wrap me and fold me in dreams when my spirit
shall know surcease.
I live and am happy, and as I live I fear not
thee, O Death.

TULIPS.

Filmy as foam and as frail as a blade
  Of Autumn-tinged grass, so they came to her
    sight,
Red, red and yellow, with varying shade
  Yellow and red, with a blending of white,—
Tulips, whose petal-tips twisted and turned,
Tulips, that reddened and smouldered and
    burned,
Flowers whose cups held the sunlight inurned.

Never a blossom as piquant as she,
  Search where you will and as long as you
    may.
Why does she come at this late day to me
  To mould me as mouldeth a potter his clay?
I, who have recked not of clouds overcast
I, who have baffled and banished the past,
To be conquered and tamed by a woman at
    last!

How do they seem in their beauty to her?
    As tulips — or germs of the Infinite plan?
Shall a flower's dumb petal in wakening stir,
    And never the heart of a woman or man?
Tulips, all dashed with the dew and the rain,
Tulips, that glow with their passionate stain,
As heart of my heart and with pain as my pain.

ON SUMMER NIGHTS.

On summer nights the yellow stars
  Shine through the watches held on high,
Suspended from the countless spars
  Of cloud-fleets anchored in the sky;
And wafted past upon the breeze
  Slow winding down from distant heights
There comes the roll of far-off seas
    On summer nights.

On summer nights the signal stars
  Flash o'er a wide, wild waste of seas,
The signal lights of ruddy Mars,
  Orion, and the Pleiades;
And down the winds a murmur sweeps
  Like whir of wings in circling flights,
The ebb and flow of mystic deeps
    On summer nights.

On summer nights the steadfast stars
   Swing from the masts of shadow ships
That lie within the harbor bars
   Where the long sea-roll curls and dips ;
And still there comes in divers keys
   Down drifting from those beacon lights
The spectral wash of far-off seas
    On summer nights.

LILIES.

Teach me but half thy purity
    And I will rest content,
Just half the spell of white-winged peace
    Which, to thy petals lent,
Makes all that 's pure and passionless
    In one deep stillness blent.

From liquid depths that give me back
    The shadows from below,
I see thy forms, all statuesque,
    Wreathed in the river's flow
That sends their still reflection up
    As white as driven snow.

Ah ! what am I to such as these, —
    Sad lilies, tall and fair ;
That stand as pale and motionless
    Amid the summer air,
As though a sculptor's marble flowers
    Were but unfolded there?

31

THE CRY OF THE TOILERS.

FAR to the clouds ascending,
Over the darkness trending,
Wailing and never ending
   Floats up a fated cry :
" Fixed in poverty's niches,
In hovels, dens, and ditches,
Starved in the midst of riches
   We die, we die, we die."

Those who have mirth and madness
Mock at the wraith of sadness,
Joy shall be theirs, and gladness
   Skies that are blue and fair ;
These shall with thirst be burning
Prone on the world's wheel turning
By the steep hillsides learning
   The lesson of despair.

32

Little their time for sleeping,
Sowing but never reaping,
Ever the vigil keeping
    Watchfully, night and day ;
Strong in their dull persistence,
Breasting the wave's resistance
Just for a bare existence, —
    So runs their world away.

Still do their hearts aspire
Yearning for something higher,
As from their souls the fire
    Of hapless craving springs ;
Scourged by the thongs and lashes
Bleeding from cruel gashes,
Crucified — upward flashes
    This cry of theirs that rings,

High in the heavens o'er us,
Resonant and sonorous,
Blending its mighty chorus
    With drifting wind and rain ;
Like to a vague outreaching
Despairing, yet beseeching,
The cry of a full heart teaching
    Its longing and its pain.

3   33

Sorrow their lips unsealing
Famine and woe revealing,
Into the midnight pealing
    Echoes the shuddering cry :
" We whom a stern fate tosses
Lone, on a sea of losses,
Christ of the thorns and crosses
    We die, we die, we die."

COW-BELLS.

I MIND me well, as a barefoot lad
　　When the toil of the day was over,
How I dropped the bars by the barnyard path
　　And walked to the dewy clover,
While far away rose the sound of bells
Faint as the murmur of sea-worn shells,
　　"Tin, tin, tin," came the echoes thin,
　　　　And then as they drifted nearer,
　　"Ting, along, ling," would the chorus ring
　　　　Through the distance clear and clearer.

And by the ford where the gray mill loomed
　　I drove them down to the edges,
And the great round moon peeped over a cloud
　　As they stood knee-deep in sedges ;
And the bells kept time in a rude refrain
Like rain-drops dashed on a window-pane,
　　"Clink, clank, clink," as they bent to drink
　　　　Where the spray from the dam came foam-
　　　　　　ing,
　　And "Clink, clink, clank," as they climbed
　　　　the bank
　　　　In the starlit, shadowy gloaming.

35

And on through the pastures back we came
　Where the cricket's rasping shrillness
Sprang up from the roots of the ribbon grass
　And dinned in the twilight stillness ;
But the jangling cow-bells drowned his cry
With discords harsh as they hurried by,
　　" Cling, clang, clong," as they swayed along
　　　With the bats and the night-hawks o'er
　　　　them,
　　And " Cling, clang, clang," how the music
　　　rang
　　As they surged by the bars before them.

And there as I raised the rough-hewn poles
　And pushed them into their sockets,
And lazily sat on the old rail fence
　With hands thrust deep in my pockets,
I listened still for a straying note,
And whiles from the dusk would softly float,
　　" Co-link," and then through the maze again
　　　In the hush of the summer weather,
　　" Co-lank " — 't was all, and in God's far hall
　　The star-choirs sang together.

36

JACK-O'-DREAMS.

You see me on the crowded street
    In some fair woman's face
One moment, then I vanish fleet
    And leave behind no trace ;
You find me in the flush of youth,
    I fill the niche of age,
And all well-known am I forsooth
    To sinner, saint, and sage.

I haunt the stars in blackest night,
    I come in noontide's gaze,
And scourge along in endless flight
    The caravan of days.
Nor cowl nor cloister shuts me out
    In beauty's arms am I,
And I am with your hope and doubt
    Your laughter and your sigh.

The wind's wild wings shall waft me down
    As long as winds do blow ;
Spring's green is mine, and Autumn's brown
    And Summer's orchard snow.
And wraith-like in its robes of mist
    My flitting form will be,
Where cold foam-serpents writhe and twist
    In Winter, by the sea.

Nay : I will pierce where spirits stand
    Beyond the soul's eclipse,
As swift as when from loosened hand
    The carrier pigeon slips ;
My shadow stays, though evermore
    Mine other self it seems ;
You follow, but I go before
    For I am Jack-o'-Dreams.

THE LOCUST.

A SOMBRE-HUED locust was singing to me —
   Seventeen years, seventeen years,
Up on a branch of the mulberry tree
   (Seventeen years and years).
The Summer was steeped in the languor of
       June
And sun-dial shadows were creeping to noon
As the locust spun out his monotonous tune —
   Of seventeen, seventeen years.

And how long ago did I hear it before?
   Seventeen years, seventeen years.
Just the same echo its resonance bore
   (Seventeen years and years).
Dead ashes of days, how they taste on the lips,
How air-castles topple and how the time slips!
Say, friend, did you hail them, my long-van-
     ished ships,
   Those seventeen, seventeen years?

39

Sing on through the summer, O locust, with
    glee, —
  Seventeen years, seventeen years.
The leaf is yet green on the mulberry tree
  (Seventeen years and years).
Since last you were here, I am cynical grown,
I 've seen the June leaves by December wind
    strown,
The world is Medusa, and turns men to stone
  In seventeen, seventeen years.

DREAMS.

Over the long, rich, billowy grass, up and down
    are the footsteps flying
  Of viewless winds that pass and leave no
    token of their flight ;
With never a tree to mar the stretch of the
    prairie around me lying,
  A dark green sea, whose rolling waves the
    sun has tipped with light.

The iron-weed sways on the wind-swept ridge,
    the wild rose blooms in the hollow,
  A hawk wheels round in circling sweep
    through trackless paths on high,
And over the grass the breezes go, and the
    tremulous echoes follow
  Filling the crannies of eddying winds from
    earth to sky.

Horizon-ward and far to the west, like the
　　smoke of a distant steamer,
　Mounting slowly up the skies, on the steps
　　of a hidden stair,
Vague, so vague, as vague and dim as the
　　dream of an idle dreamer
　A curling cloud-wraith, spiral formed, is
　　rising through the air.

Sun and wind, and the far-off sky; the sun
　　that shines and the wind that passes;
　The life that is, and beyond the clouds the
　　life that is to be —
Dreams, all dreams, that come and go, as the
　　wind's light footprints over the grasses
　What is my life but a drop of rain that falls
　　in a shoreless sea?

SONGS UNSUNG.

Sweet the song of the thrush at dawning,
　　When the grass lies wet with spangled dew ;
Sweet the sound of the brook's low whisper
　　Mid reeds and rushes wandering through ;
Clear and pure is the west wind's murmur
　　That croons in the branches all day long ;
But the songs unsung are the sweetest music
　　And the dreams that die are the soul of song.

The fairest hope is the one which faded,
　　The brightest leaf is the leaf that fell ;
The song that leaped from the lips of sirens
　　Dies away in an old sea-shell.
Far to the heights of viewless fancy
　　The soul's swift flight like a swallow goes,
For the note unheard is the bird's best carol
　　And the bud unblown is the reddest rose.

Deepest thoughts are the ones unspoken,
    That only the heart sense, listening, hears ;
Most great joys bring a touch of silence
    Greatest grief is in unshed tears.
What we hear is the fleeting echo.
    A song dies out, but a dream lives on ;
The rose-red tints of the rarest morning
    Are lingering yet in a distant dawn.

Somewhere, dim in the days to follow
    And far away in the life to be,
Passing sweet, is a song of gladness, —
    The spirit-chant of the soul set free.
Chords untouched are the ones we wait for —
    That never rise from the harp unstrung :
We turn our steps to the years beyond us,
    And listen still for the songs unsung.

OUTDOORS.

.

MY MOTHER EARTH.

I.

INTO the silence of thy temples green
To thy dear arms, O mother earth I come
When sore distressed from life's perplexing ills,
And steep my soul in thy all-healing strength.
As wounded denizens of wood and field
Seek thy most quiet and secluded depths,
So I, when racked by lingering heart-aches go
Into those wide and leafy halls of thine
And give myself to solitude and thee.

I am a worshipper at thy fair shrines
O mother mine ; in Nature's ritual
Thy forms are to me as an open book.
I read thy future, present, and thy past
By many a curious and half-hidden sign
And trace thy wanderings throughout the years
With knowledge quaffed at thy perennial founts.
And most I love the dim autumnal woods ;
Dear friends, tho' silent, the companion trees,
That whisper as I pass, and scatter down
Leaf benedictions on my leaf-strewn path, —
Old oaks, colossal, that like sowers stand

Amid the acorns scattered on the ground ;
Maples, whose garments of sun-tinted flame
Seem gorgeous banners in October's van ;
And pines, like fingers that point up to
   heaven,
That distant land beyond the purple clouds.

I know the windings of down-flowing streams
The mossy logs that stretch from bank to bank
And shallows carpeted with pebbles bright,
Where bubbles in the sunlight flash and gleam ;
I know the texture of the gray squirrel's nest
The drumming of the partridge, and the cry
That comes when darting o'er the ripples past
The lone kingfisher speeds his sudden flight.

Trust me to know the secrets of thy house,
Dear mother earth ! in thy deep niches placed
The primrose waves, and slender violets
Smile dewily to greet the south wind's kiss.
Am I not known to all thy family ?
And may I not in thy most inner dells
Find the quick welcome of thy sympathy ?
My mother earth, mine ancient mother earth,
Dear is to me thy wintry garb of gray
Dear the green splendor of thy April crown,
Sweet the soft whispers of thy summer breeze
And doubly dear thy rich October dreams.

The sunshine on the tree-trunks comes to
    weave
Strange draperies of rare and antique lace
In web-like lines slow filtered through the
    leaves;
Cloud-land peeps down from blue, serenest
    skies,
The earth's heart beats from slow pulsating
    breast,
And freshest greenwood odors fill the air
With incense from a hidden censer swung.

There 's not a vein upon the tiniest leaf
Nor cobweb silvered by the glistening dews
Nor bird-wing brushing through the forest
    aisles,
But what I see and feel its influence.
Why, all the paintings that were ever praised
And all the music struck from vibrant strings
Are but a faint reflection of the woods,
The mimicry of art at Nature's feet.

In the deep silence of autumnal shades
Old sorrows die, new memories spring up,
Hope, like a torch, illuminates the road,
And all our former burdens fall away.

Vistas and valleys of rich-colored woods
Wave high above the sylvan thickets dense ;
And there, when straying footsteps lightly fall
Shy wood-birds flit, across the space between,
And timid rabbits lift expectant ears.

O mother earth, my constant love for thee,
Born of the very earliest of my thoughts,
Holds in its scope no taint of worldly things.
Thy changing moods are but the different
    lights
Of constancy that lives forevermore ;
For all things else are frail as ropes of sand
Beside the truth and beauty of thy face.

O mother earth, thy leaves and trees and
    streams
The large content that fills thy sleeping woods
Thy calm repose, and heart-consoling balm
Are more than all religions are to me ;
And almost half a Druid now am I
As in thy arms, on mossy couch outstretched,
Forsaking trouble to the wayward winds,
I give my soul to spirit hands unseen
And drift away to dreamland through thy
    gates.

OCTOBER.

A MAZE of leaves in a rich mosaic,
   Brown and yellow and flaming red,
Where the winds go by in the depths archaic
   And bright through the branches overhead
Like a fair white hand at a window shutter
   The sunlight under the leaf-shades peeps,
Now here, now there, with its changing flutter,
   While below the old earth sleeps and sleeps.

A fringe of gray and a sweep of yellow
   Crimson streaks and a belt of brown,
Mingled in with the sunshine mellow
   And sun-tinged leaves soft floating down ;
White the gleam of the shining pebbles
   And green the moss on the banks beside,
As down the shallows the buoyant bubbles
   Into the cool wood shadows glide.

Deep in the heart of the woods lies glowing
   The gathered life of a thousand noons,
And echoes faint through the trees are blowing
   As mystic Æolus plays his tunes,
And the passing step of the wind god rouses
   The dreaming leaves as he hurries by,
While the sunshine droops and the still air
      drowses
   Under the purpling autumn sky.

Fleecy clouds by the wind swept over,
   And a vague, faint scent all sharp and sweet,
Like the mingled smell of thyme and clover
   Bruised by the summer's flying feet ;
Ashes, fires, and dying embers,
   A waste of gold and a vault of flame,
And the frail gray ghosts of the lost Septembers
   Vanishing, fading, past reclaim.

ON THE HILLS

THE tangled grass is at her feet
  The blue sky distant stands,
And shadows on its marge repeat
  The spell of weaving hands.

Wide vaults of freest space beyond
  To her clear eyes are shown,
And where the breeze has waved its wand
  Light thistle-downs up-blown.

A hawk in widening circle sails
  Above the far-off trees,
And motionless amid the swales
  The cattle stand at ease.

She marks the yellow stubbles shorn
  As on her way she takes ;
And shore-lines of September corn
  On which the sunlight breaks.

The day her forehead kisses fair
  The wind her long locks thrills ;
Diana of the ruddy hair
  Tall-striding o'er the hills.

53

A SONG OF THE DUST.

A SONG of the good gray dust
   That lay in the winding road,
Till caught by a sudden gust
   It sprang from its dry abode,
And over the hills was sowed
   On the leaves and ribbon-grass,
On the gilded wheat, and the shady sheet
   Of the swamp-pool, smooth as glass.

A song of the good gray dust
   That falls on flower and thorn,
That powders the sumach's rust
   And whitens the bladed corn ;
That drops in the ways forlorn
   Or rests on the blossoms white,
As a wayward touch that has taught thus much
   Of the wind's æolian flight.

A song of the good gray dust
  That tinges the wayside leaf,
That hangs in a tawny crust
  On the farmer's home-bound sheaf,
That swings for a moment brief
  On the barley's bearded sheen,
Till the creaking peals of the wagon-wheels
  Shall scatter it down between.

A song of the good gray dust
  Ground out from the trampled clod,
And into the highway thrust
  Where the lone wayfarers plod ;
Yet still, by the grace of God,
  Shall it feel the cooling rain
And shall know the bliss of the wind's light
    kiss
  That stoops to the country lane.

A CALIFORNIA IDYL.

A ROAD-RUNNER dodged in the chaparral
   As a coin will slip from the hand of a wizard
A black wasp droned by his sun-baked cell,
   While flat on a stone lay a Nile-green lizard,
And a wolf in the rift of a sycamore
Sat gray as a monk at the mission door.

A sage-hen scratched 'mong the cactus spike
   And high in the sky was the noon sun's
      glamour,
While steady as ever rose anvil-strike
   Came the rat-tat-tat of a yellow-hammer,
And a shy quail lowered his crested head
To the dust-lined sweep of a dry creek's bed.

And out of the earth a tarantula crept
   On his hairy legs to the road's white level,
With eyes where a demon's malice slept
   And the general air of an unchained devil,
While a rattlesnake by the dusty trail
Lay coiled in a mat of mottled scale.

Then the gray wolf sprang on the sage-hen
    there,
  And the lizard snapped at the wasp and
    caught him,
While the spider fled to his sheltering lair
  As though a shadowy foeman sought him,
And the road-runner slipped from the wayside
    brake
And struck his beak through the rattlesnake.

ﺍ

THE CATBIRD'S WHISTLE.

An old bridge stood with dust thick strewn,
Where through a crooked country lane
A brook flowed down, and out again
Slow gurgling past with quiet croon ;
While sunshine kissed the cool gray stones
And chequered every leaf and spray,
And shallows sang, in treble tones,
Where pebbles in mosaic lay.

And softly, from the deepest shade,
A catbird's whistle low and clear
Crept out as though the sound was made
For only Nature's listening ear ;
Like dripping water falling slow
Round mossy rocks in music rare,
So, mellowed by the summer glow
The catbird's whistle echoed there.

58

Far up along the short green sward
The white sheep nibbled at the grass,
And lightly, as the winds did pass
Would come the catbird's minor chord, —
A call that made all others mute,
Soft thrilling thro' the drowsy air ;
As some lost note from Orpheus' lute
So came the catbird's whistle there.

EN SILHOUETTE.

THE blot on the spider's murky web,
The sombre shade where the ripples ebb,
  And the darkness through the trees,
But never a shadow that falls so far
As when o'er the ruddy western bar
The sunset sails by the first gray star
    Into the twilight seas.

The tawny leaves that are floating down
The trailing vines that are crisp and brown
  As grass on the darkling leas ;
A lone harp strung in the swarthy reeds
That sounds its chords as the north wind leads
Where the dusky water slow recedes
    Into the twilight seas.

The hills in the distance, black as jet,
A burned-out sun that is sinking yet,
  The sigh of a restless breeze —
And who shall mourn for the days now sped,
The after-glow of a summer dead,
Long since with the far-down shadows fled,
    Into the twilight seas ?

A MARCH SUNSET.

FAINT clouds that form a snowy ledge,
  And through the space that twilight fills
The gray half-moon with battered edge
  Sailing athwart the sunken hills.

And in the west a ragged glint
  Of sunset splendor sends its flash
Where night and day, like steel to flint,
  All suddenly together clash.

And down the chill wind's rustling flight
  From out a waste of desert sky
Sinks, bubbling into vasty night,
  A wandering curlew's cry.

HICKORY LILIES.

Lo! where the gray of early March
   Lies frost-like on the grasses green,
And by the roadway many an arch
   Of tangled branch and vine is seen,
Weird flowers upon old Winter's tomb
The waxen hickory lilies bloom.

Soft, sensuous petals pale as death
   With drooping edges half uncurled
Unwavering in the wind's cool breath
   That drifts across the upper world ;
Strange forest-buds that gleam o'erhead
Their creamy pallor splotched with red.

The mist from out the marsh below
   Spreads filmy wings and glides away ;
Burns in the east a ruddier glow,
   While high above the hillside clay
All wet with dew, the dawn's perfume
The waxen hickory lilies bloom.

THE AMATEUR PHOTOGRAPHER.

THERE was a wandering scientist went by,
  And gleaned odd bits of Nature with his
      lens, —
Far woods dark outlined on an April sky
  And stately cat-tails by the reedy fens ;
  And streams that trickled through the nar-
      row glens
That in the northern wildernesses lie.

Here lay a stretch of sleeping water, there
  The sunset's rose, its petals curling down ;
And sometimes rock-ribbed cliffs rose gaunt
      and bare,
  With massive broken pillars rough and
      brown
  Where the dim twilight in her nun-like gown
Came stealing in upon the drowsy air.

And these were all dream-glances, till the sun
  Flashed in upon his camera, and set
A vision of a vision, from a net

Of sunlit strands all in an instant spun,
And thus at length the subtle toil was done:
Frail frost-work, mocking Nature, black as jet.

But oh! when through their transformation
    came
    These sombre plates, how wonderful were
        wrought
Deep pools that darkened in a woodland frame,
    And rippling currents that the light had
        caught,
    With leaf flotillas on their windings brought
Crisp-curled mementos of the sunlight's flame.

And glimpses of the stars and gnarly trees;
    The moon's slow splendor and the hopeful
        grass;
And winy tints of August where the lees
    Of summer sank, like bubbles in a glass,
    And clouds high castled in a snowy mass
Over a voiceless waste of azure seas.

The color was not there, for those who sought
    The color of the senses; but the wise,
By keen imagination erstwhile taught
    Saw all the wealth of Nature's myriad dyes,

And gazing still, with introspective eyes,
Found tints that those not dreamers held for
    naught.

The music was not there, — the first faint notes
    That morning brings when dawn-announcing
        birds
Pipe warily from half-unwilling throats ;
    Nor yet was there the lowing of the herds ;
    Nor came across the water spoken words
From the still figures in the dusky boats.

And yet 't was all so vivid, fresh, and strong,
    The feeling of the music, that it seemed
To move with you as move the winds along,
    To ripple up wherever water gleamed,
    And soothed you with its fancies as you
        dreamed
Until the very silence seemed a song,

And all the shores of summer's sunlit deeps
    Seemed etched against the blue-horizoned
        days,
And broad reflections of the cloudy steeps
    Swept idly down across the meadow ways :
    For this was Nature, seen as through a haze
As when one dreams of pictures while he
        sleeps.

VIOLETS.

THE fields are wrapped in mantles white
  Of glittering, drifted snow,
The earth's quick summer pulse is gone
  Yet, beating dim and slow,
Her muffled throbs come welling up
  From distant depths below.

It cannot be the days are dead
  Though frozen are the streams ;
For in the sun's dull winter light
  A promised summer gleams,
And what are winter's wraiths at last
  But ghosts of summer dreams ?

Dream on, dream on, dear mother earth
  Till April's fire shall glow !
Still in my heart thy spring-tide swells
  In endless ebb and flow ;
I see as with prophetic eyes
  The violets in the snow.

66

AN INDIAN SUMMER DAY.

I saw the East's pale cheek blush rosy red
When from his royal palace in the sky,
The sun-god, clothed in crimson splendor, came
And lit the torch of day with sudden flame,
While morning on white wings flew swiftly by
Bringing a message that the night was dead.

High noon, and not a murmur in the streams;
And silence fills the hazy autumn air;
Sun-painted leaves drift slowly to the ground
Amid a quiet, soft and yet profound
And lie in russet windrows scattered there, —
All Nature in a misty slumber dreams.

And then upon the close of dying day
Softly and silently as falling snow,
The twilight comes in dusky folds and rings
And over all a darkling shadow flings ;
High overhead a star begins to glow
And cow-bells tinkle faintly, far away.

ISIS.

I AM whatever is ; for day by day
   I sparkle in each flower's richest hue,
   And with a lavish hand I scatter dew
When twilight comes in mantle dim and gray.

My spirit shines in every faithful star ;
   My voice is heard in all the winds that pass ;
   My name is written on each blade of grass
And in all climes my leafy castles are.

Earth, sea, and sky, and what are they but me ?
   Each cloud-capped mountain or each grain
      of sand ?
   I paint the shells on an untrodden strand
Where whispers low the long-sought Northern
      sea.

I am whatever has been ; in the dust
   Of shattered empires and of levelled thrones
   My presence stands, — ay, even mid the
      bones
Of coffined kings, and in their armor rust.

Where the unnumbered dead are, there am I.
  Where ivy creeps along the churchyard
      mould ;
  I gleam in the pale moonlight shining cold
On ghostly stones where tears are never dry.

I am the voice of centuries ; my hand
  Holds life and death, all mystery, all fate ;
  My secrets told to only those who wait
My domain infinite o'er sea and land.

I am whatever shall be ; though the night
  Be changed to day, though stars their courses
      fail,
  My giant forces like great vessels sail
Unharmed, impregnable, in conscious might.

In the long years that shall hereafter come
  I will be found by forest field and stream
  Still reigning o'er the universe supreme,
Forever speaking, yet forever dumb.

All darkly, darkly, in the gloom I hide
  And oh ! so brightly in the sunbeams shine,
  All changes and all great emotions mine
And in my strength and beauty calmly bide.

The veil that hides my face has ever cast
　　A dazzling shadow on the path of years,
　　The hope and dread with mingled joy and
　　　　tears
Of those who solve my mystery at last.

Peace, restless heart : 't is not for mortal breath
　　To breathe the ether of the inner skies,
　　And no man's hand can lift the veil that lies
Between the tragedies of life and death.

THE MEADOW-LARK.

A SEA of grass on either side
The prairie stretches far and wide,
Its undulating line of blades
Reflects the noontide lights and shades,
And brings before me one by one
The pictures wrought by wind and sun.

And silence reigns, save for the breeze
And muffled hum of droning bees,
Till in the summer hush I hear
A prairie signal sweet and clear,
In mournful, piercing notes that mark
The whistle of the meadow-lark.

Like one wild cry for loved and lost
From some lone spirit tempest-tossed,
It wails across the waving grass,
And, blending with the winds that pass,
It scatters echoes at my feet
So full of pain, so deadly sweet.

Oh ! heart of hearts, could my unrest
Find such a song within my breast,
My passionate and yearning cry
Would echo on from sea to sky,
Along the path of future years,
And touch the listening world to tears.

SONG.

THE deft Musician's fingers
  Lo ! they lie crossed and numb,
And the soul of the violin is dead
  And the magic strings are dumb.

Closed is the old piano
  And chordless its amber keys,
As the vanished tidal murmurs
  Of prehistoric seas.

The singer's voice is silent
  That once was sweet and strong,
They faded out like a wild-bird's note, —
  The singer and his song.

The maestro's touch dies with him ;
  'T is gone for good or ill ;
And the singer's lips no echoes leave
  To linger with us still.

And only the runes of Nature
  Abide with us for long,
And only the wind and ripples
  Sing the eternal song.

73

IN THE HEART OF THE HICKORY TREE.

THERE is never a blossom of Spring alive
 There is never a bud, he said ;
The cruel snows through the branches drive
 And the leaves and grass are dead ;
But the pulse of the world beat on below
 In spite of the North wind's dree,
And a bead of sap lay all aglow
 In the heart of the hickory tree.

There is never a rose to bloom, he cried,
 Nor the ghost of a lily tall,
Nor a morning-glory streaked and pied
 To smile from the garden wall ;
But a seed that slept in the frosty earth
 Held colors all fair to see,
And the bead of sap bubbled up with mirth
 In the heart of the hickory tree.

There is never a stalk of green, I wis,
　Again to himself he said,
No primrose pale for the winds to kiss —
　He sighed, and he shook his head ;
Yet the snows were only the late-month rains,
　And March came following free,
And the sap oozed down through the hidden
　　　veins
　In the heart of the hickory tree.

There is never a bird in the thickets now,
　Nor a ripple upon the creek,
Nor a leaf, he said, on the apple-bough
　However I wait or seek ;
But a violet under the frozen clay
　Dreamed on of the days to be,
And a bud was born that very morn
　In the heart of the hickory tree.

DEFIANCE.

I QUESTION whether 't is worth the trouble
    The toil and travail, the sin and pain ;
For who that blows but a painted bubble
    Shall grasp it to him and call it gain ?
And the life you live, be it high or humble,
    Is quickly under the grasses hid
As into a narrow niche you tumble,
    And the clods fall thick on your coffin-lid.

The light of love and the spark of passion
    Shall flame on the lips and die away,
The lips once red that are now turned ashen
    And sunk so soon into yesterday ;
I lift my voice in a measured scorning
    Against the Gods that they raise on high,
And dawn bring dusk, and the night bring
       morning
    I care not whether I live or die.

I knew the touch of a child's soft finger
  But lost its clasp when I loved her best
I marked in June where the young birds linger
  But the snow soon covered an empty nest ;
And I tell you spite of your strong endeavor
  The vision melts and the fabric fails,
While all that we are is passing ever
  Like dead leaves whirled in the Autumn
    gales.

I turn my face to the glass of Nature
  And dip my feet in her streams again,
And verse myself in her nomenclature
  Reading her heart as the hearts of men ;
And I know she leads where the Gods must
    follow
  The seas survive though the creeds will pass,
And the words of man seem poor and hollow
  To a grain of sand or a blade of grass.

A few score years, and the race is ended
  And we from the world are outward thrust,
And each with his mother-earth is blended
  Ashes to ashes, and dust to dust,
Save here and there where the high soul sunders
  A dread command while the rest stand dumb,
And daring the strength of Jove's own thunders
  Steals fire from heaven for those to come.

POETA NASCITUR, NON FIT.

AND dost thou think to tempt the muse
By such vain arts as lovers use?

And wilt thou bring her learnèd thought
In cunning form of rhythm wrought?

And wilt thou mould in rigid rules
Cold fables from the classic schools?

Do all of this, and then how long
Will sound the echo of thy song?

No longer than shall tremble in
A cracked and shattered violin

Some chord-wave loosened by the bow
That fades in briefest tremolo.

Why! teach the lark to sing by note,
And Pan to play his reeds by rote,

But never hope Parnassian height
By Art's mere imitative flight.

78

Nay ! dive thou deep in Nature's heart,
And tear her leaves and grass apart ;

Wander thou forth in sun and rain
To tread the paths of joy and pain ;

Live, toil, and strive, and keenly scan
The mystery of thy fellow-man ;

And, most of all, know thou the spell
Of Love's high heaven and dungeoned hell,—

And then, if on thy natal morn
A singer's soul was in thee born,

Perchance the anguish may be thine
To touch the lips of song divine.

THRENODY.

THE roving hawk will find his mate
  And stars companions be,
But I, — I only stand and wait, —
  There is no mate for me.

The stranger rivers meeting blend
  And journey to the sea ;
I have, mayhap, a single friend
  But none who watch for me.

Nor woman's kiss hath bound me fast
  Nor creed hath bent my knee ;
The fields, and blue skies overcast, —
  These are enough for me.

Alone, unsolved, I bide my time
  Till death shall set me free,
A man whose lips were steeped in rhyme, —
  Oh, dreamers, pray for me !

80

WARP AND WOOF.

THE KING'S LOVE AND HATE.

"OH! King," a courtier cried,
As low obeisance made he,
" Whom hatest thou the most ?"
The King replied,
" Those who already have betrayed me."

" This question then I bring,
Whom lov'st thou most, I pray thee ?"
" With my best love I love "
So said the King —
" Those who hereafter will betray me."

THE MESSAGE OF THE TOWN.

LOOK up to the stony arches
Where art and mammon meet,
There 's a sound where Traffic marches
A call in the City street,
 For a voice is ever ringing
 " Gird up your loins and flee
 I will harden your heart or break it
 If you will abide with me."

Go forth with a noble yearning,
Give heed to the griefs of men,
And the years will find you turning
To that mocking voice again,
 Which ever recurrent whispers
 Like the chant of the restless sea
 " I will harden your heart or break it
 If you will abide with me."

No time for the touch of gladness
Nor yet for the boon of tears,
We toss in a cloud of madness
Whirled round by the whirling years
    And an echo lingers always
    From which we are never free
    " I will harden your heart or break it
    If you will abide with me."

Aye I carve it in iron letters
High over your widest gate,
Since we all must wear the fetters
Who seek the appointed fate,
    And the winds shall bring the message
    Through all of the days that be
    " I will harden your heart or break it
    If you will abide with me."

" L'ALLEGRO."

A RED light on the Tiber came
   From scarlet banners waved on high ;
A city wrapped in smoke and flame,
   With blazing columns lit the sky.

Above the tramp of rushing feet,
   And o'er the conflagration's din,
Arose, in measure sharp and sweet,
   The music of a violin.

THE PROMPTER.

FROM underneath the stage's floor
A man steps upward through a door,
Leaving behind the shrilling din
Of cello tuned, and violin,
And hears across the building vast
One·far, faint flute-note ripple past.

Within the wings he takes his stand
His well-thumbed book in lean right hand,
And pieces out from page to page
The fool's broad jest or tyrant's rage,
The lover's lisp, the lady's sigh
And headlong warrior's battle-cry.

Not his to mouth the motley lines
A man of gestures, and of signs;
Of humble port and modest mien
With presence hardly felt or seen,
And yet whose long forefinger gives
The cue to him who dies or lives.

Not his to mark the long-drawn pause,
The silence — and the wild applause
When nature, through the actor's art
Smiles in on each awakened heart,
For though all others have their share
None heeds the patient prompter there.

I cry you mercy ; by God's rood,
When death has stripped them, prone and nude,
When each to heaven turns his brow
This prompter shall not rate as now,
But as a man, among the men,
Be reckoned with the faithful then.

APPLE-BLOSSOMS.

NOT apple-blossoms for the old home's sake;
The hill-side farm, the orchard vistas fair,
Youth, hope, and mother, all my treasures
    there
Not apple-blossoms, lest my heart should
    break.

THE WRAITH OF LOCHBURY.

Gray battlements of ancient stone,
With clinging ivy overgrown,
And granite towers rising free
Above the night-imprisoned sea,
Announced in stern and rugged mien
The feudal castle of MacLean.

And up and down the gloomy shore
A spectral steed his rider bore,
As through the night, with haunting cry,
A wailing horseman galloped by
Along the lonely ocean sands,
And beat his breast with fleshless hands.

Far, far away, 'neath Spanish skies,
A Scottish chieftain dying lies,
And with his glazing eyes he sees
His castle walls, while on the breeze
He hears a wailing, moaning cry,
And phantom hoof-beats gallop by.

THE SPHINX.

Couched in the dull Egyptian sands, dumb,
  and yet with a voice pathetic
That seems to come from the stony lips, that
  ever seems to say :
" I am a part of the old-world life, of a buried
  age prophetic.
I am a rock that the waves of time will
  never wear away.

" Out of the bygone years I gaze, desertward,
  and my meditation
Sees a fold of the tawny sands, where once
  was a palace tall ;
And I hear the heart of the great world beat,
  in swinging, slow pulsation ;
The great world's heart that throbs the same
  though Pharaohs rise and fall.

" Kings and queens and the nations all, fading
out in the dust together,
And centuries long that vanished in 'to-morrow' and 'to-day':
For each gray age has floated past as light as
an ibis feather,
Since I was hewn, and left alone, in these
sad wastes to stay.

" And in the visions that come to me thro' the
curtains rent asunder
That hide the years — I have heard a sound,
all rhythmical and vast ;
The mail-clad tread of mighty hosts — like a
measured roll of thunder,
The tramp of the Caesar's legions, the
Romans marching past.

"This, all this, I see and hear, in the sun and
moon and night winds blowing,
In sunset fire, and in the moon, the sheen of
whose silver disc,
Is scattering down the cold white rays on
Nilus softly flowing,
And searching out the pictured scenes on
ruin and obelisk.

" Come what come may, or sun or storm, the
river's calm or the desert's bleakness
And still I couch in the shifting sands and
watch the years alone,
Holding within my giant grasp the strength of
art and the sculptor's weakness,
The man who died — the thought that lived
in everlasting stone."

HE TRAVELS THE FASTEST WHO TRAVELS ALONE.

THE stirrup-cup's drained and the messenger
    flown —
He travels the fastest who travels alone.

A shout of " God speed you," the gleam of a
    spur
And the hearth-flame behind sinks away in a
    blur.

A form in the darkness that fades on the sight
And the clatter of hoofs as he rides through
    the night.

Not a star overhead, nor a neighboring lamp
Save the fire-fly's glimmer in marsh-vistas damp,

Or a spark where the horse-shoe strikes sharp
    on a stone,
He travels the fastest who travels alone.

And onward and onward each long mile is
    passed
With the echo of horses' hoofs following fast,

Till the gray light of dawn o'er the highway
he sees
And a crowd and a scaffold loom black through
the trees.

When with foam from the charger white-
flecking his sleeve
He spurs him still faster, wild crying, "Re-
prieve!"

And death like a feather now backward is
blown
He travels the fastest who travels alone.

AN OLD DAGUERREOTYPE.

Two clear, grave eyes, that wondering look
From some forgotten long ago ;
A childish face that cannot know
The secrets hidden in the book
Of future years,
The care and toil, the busy strife,
The joys that jewel every life,
The tears.

From that lost time — from childhood-land —
The wistful, speaking, hazel eyes
Look out as on unclouded skies ;
Where glowing hopes rise hand in hand,
And sunshine streams
Along the path of breaking day,
While all the shadows fade away,
Like dreams.

Thus kept by art's all-saving grace
Peeps from a distant hazy nook
Of time gone by this sunny look
Upon a young, untroubled face,
That holds within
The boyish eyes, those limpid springs —
No taint of earth or earthly things,
No sin.

A PRODIGAL.

I HAVE marked the gleam of the ploughshare
  And known of the sweat of toil,
Where the breath from the horses' nostrils
    puffed
  And the inky curve of soil,
Rolled away in undulations
  As a black-snake leaves his coil.

When the axe in the timber sounded
  And the wedge and the frizzled maul,
Had found the heart of many an oak
  And many a hickory tall ;
Where branching woodland giants crashed
  Down thundering to their fall.

I have watched the paling starlight
  As a sign of the task begun,
And my feet were wet by the midnight dews
  And my brow by the midday sun,
Till the harvest moon in the southern skies
  Made shift for a day's work done.

I have sat in the herder's saddle
　In the sleet and the blinding rain,
And heard the roll of hurrying hoofs
　Beat time on a hollow plain,
And whoso works with a strenuous hand
　Has labored not in vain.

And at last in a towered city
　Scarce more than a boy I stood,
Where the smoke hung over the steeples
　Like the folds of a witch's hood;
And life was a sea before me
　Where those survived who could.

But I breasted the coming billows
　And swept their crests aside,
And never a sea or dark or deep
　Could drown me in its tide;
And held my peace and made no moan
　Where some, I think, had died.

And each for himself I found it
　However you stay or seek,
And bitter the strife as in olden days
　When Greek met face to Greek;
And whatever it meant for the strongest
　God pity the young and weak.

Yet ever a will sustained me
  When even Love did fail,
And made my soul as strong as though
  I had looked on the Holy Grail,
And the deadliest arrow Fate could launch
  Fell blunted from its mail.

And always an eagle-spirit
  That walls could not confine,
And the bane of the three temptations
  Of woman, song, and wine,
And the husks of a keen repentance
  The bed with the sodden swine.

And or ever a God seemed distant
  In my direst hour of need,
Or the woman's hand I leaned upon
  Had pierced like the broken reed,
Or I passed with lip still thirsting
  From the cup of an empty creed,

Then I turned to the one true solace
  On life's wide battlefield,
A pride as the pride of Lucifer's
  Which dared but did not yield —
And whoso has it at its best
  Lacks neither sword nor shield.

And each to his own accounting
    I stand prepared for mine,
When death shall call for volunteers
    To step from the foremost line ;
And none will go more hopefully
    Nor with lighter heart than mine.

And he who shrinks 'neath the lash of Fate
    I hold is a base-born clod,
And my steps bend not to a Father's house
    Nor yet to the house of God,
For the strength of pride doth still abide
    To spurn the chastening rod.

ACCURSED.

From zone to zone, from east to west
In all the lands of sun and snow,
My weary footsteps to and fro
Through laggard centuries have pressed,
And evermore by land and sea
A haunting vision follows me,
By night and day.

Upon the cloud-arched stage of Time
The curtain'd years roll to the skies ;
And there before my dazzled eyes
A thorn-crowned Presence stands sublime.
I hear a voice — I hear it now —
In ringing accents, "Tarry thou
Until I come !"

ISHMAEL.

Upon my vow I stand or fall,
    Lo! here am I alone,
My hand against the hands of all
    And theirs against my own ;
My roof the stars, my bed the sod,
    The desert-home for me,
No hope nor fear of man or God
    So be it, let it be.

My hairy sandals on my feet,
    My dagger in my hand,
With shaggy courser eagle-fleet
    To skim the level sand.
The quiver o'er my shoulder hung
    The bow across it bent,
My gage against the whole world flung
    And so I rest content.

I know not, I, the touch of grief,
  Of pity or of tears ;
Nor heed as much as falling leaf
  The passing of the years ;
Long since Death sealed my early vow
  And often shall again,
Time stamps no Cain-mark on my brow
  For these vile sons of men.

Cold in the cloudless sky above
  Float the eternal stars,
And cold my breath to thoughts of love
  But 'neath my battle-scars
Leaps the red blood in warmth elate
  To meet my hated foe,
As forth I rush to seek my fate
  With dagger and with bow.

The blood of man has stained my hands
  My heart has turned to stone.
I roam a scourge along the sands,
  A king without a throne.
The very lion shuns my path,
  And legends utter when
I raised my voice in first-time wrath
  Against the sons of men.

MAGDALEN.

HAD she sold herself for lucre, were it but by
    the laws of man
She had reigned it proudly and royally and had
    never known the ban,
For the world can bend and stoop and cringe
    to a married courtesan.

The doors of the temples shut her out that
    welcome the righteous in
And she sits by a homeless hearth and waits
    with ghosts of might-have-been,
And the Pharisees in the market-place will
    tell you of her sin.

And still where the earth's broad highways
    * trend she weaves her lingering spell
As a spider weaves his filmy web and lurks in
    an inner cell
And her feet go down to death they say, and
    her steps take hold on hell.

But choose from a thousand maxims wise,
    fine-sifted through wisdom's sieve
And never a one will teach mankind the sound
    of the word "forgive,"
Yet this for her arts and her blandishments —
    how else is she to live?

And there's never a man shall raise his voice
    to speak for Magdalen,
And never a woman will take her hand nor
    teach her hope again ;
Who recks of the Man of Calvary when the
    church has said "Amen"?

RE-INCARNATION.

A CHILD, he played as other children do,
Mourned not the old, nor reckoned of the new.

A man, he strove with dogma and with creed
To solve the problem of the spirit's need.

Then old age came, and made him as a child,
With earth and God and all things reconciled.

THE LOST SOULS.

In vast mid-space, upon a cloudy steep
The lost souls gathered, as apart from all
Where looking downward they could see the
      pall
Of floating smoke o'er Satan's donjon keep,
And gazing upward through an azure deep
They marked the outlines of the jasper wall
That circled Eden, and the towers tall
Where golden chimes sank fitfully to sleep.

These were the souls who, living, loved and
      lost,
But after life had sought and claimed their own
And fled with them in starry realms to dwell,
And side by side along the heights they crossed
'Mid the white lilies of the moon outblown
Not needing Heaven and not fearing Hell.

SUNSET.

A RIVER'S shores — the current's sweep be-
    tween
Flecked with dead leaves; while here and
    there a stone
Rears its rude bulk against the ripples thrown;
In shadowy stretch of undulating green
The broad banks lie, and further on the sheen
Of purple thickets fleetingly is shown;
And o'er the placid waters brooding lone
Twilight and Darkness, weird twin-sisters lean.

And one still pool as slow the day declines,
Holds close the sunset's glory in its deeps
In colors that no mortal tongue could name;
And now as night comes etched in dusky lines
Low in the limpid water fitful sleeps
One last red gleam that shimmers like a flame.

LILITH.

I, WANDERING in a certain waste alone
In lands deserted, where no wild bird called,
Before the desolation stood appalled
That stretched away in dreary monotone ;
The wind went muttering like a withered crone
And stunted trees in grayish moss were shawled,
A marshy mist, slow moving, upward crawled
And sullen nature brooded, turned to stone.

But on a sudden by a swampy space
In weaving lines of breezy disarray,
A host of saffron lilies thronged the air,
And I bethought me of a woman's face
As fair, as sweet, as languorous as they,
The sunlight on her tangled yellow hair.

SONNET TO MUSIC.

I ASK not meat, a little bread will do
And cup of water dipped from some clear
    stream
Where lazily the ripples croon and dream
Adown the shining cresses slipping through ;
No more than this, for when Pan comes to woo
The silence with his pipings, then I seem
To lose myself in rapture, as I deem
Were lost, long since, Ulysses and his crew ;
For as the western winds go rustling by
O'er treetops tall and rushes sere and bent
And herd-boy brown with willow-whistle dry
Shrills out his tunes through the lone meadow
    sent
Then fill mine eyes to blindness there for I —
Give me but music and I rest content.

111

MIDNIGHT AT SEA.

TALL rise the mighty masts, while ashen sails,
Distended by the fast increasing breeze
Throw ghostly shades upon the heaving seas ;
The glittering moon alternate shines and pales
And fraught with ancient echoes of the gales
The cordage sighs, like wind-swept forest
    trees ;
And then with one long swerve the vessel frees
Her form from all the shadows, as she scales
A giant steep, while down the moonlight pours ;
And on and on the myriad billows roll
In endless race across the pulsing deeps,
Until at last where far Australia sleeps,
Each wave falls headlong on the sandy shores
Like a spent runner sinking at the goal.

THE SPINNING DERVISH.

HE wears a turban round his head
And on his feet are pointed shoes,
While from his waist a skirt outspread
Such as the tawny Arabs use
Describes a circle from his hips
And rustles like a lady's fan,
His teeth gleam whitely 'twixt his lips —
The silent Oriental man.

Then slow he turns from left to right
His arms outstretched, long, lean and browned
By suns that on Sahara smite,
And round and round and round and round
He moves in circles slow unfurled
From where his journey first began,
Like dust upon the desert whirled
The silent Oriental man.

Round, round and round, my eyes grow dim ;
His whirling figure seems to change,
The very earth goes round with him
Forsooth ! but this is passing strange,
A broken glimpse of twisting heels
And ornaments of beaten brass,
I catch, as round the Dervish reels
While one by one the minutes pass.

The half-hour wanes ; and on he spins
With hands uplifted, clenched and still,
A mighty maze of outs and ins
Impelled by weird fanatic will,
In cloudless skies the far sun burns
And shadows lengthen by a span,
While round and round and round he turns
The silent Oriental man.

So are we all from God's right hand
Sent spinning into boundless space,
And when upright we cannot stand
Death comes and thus we lose our place.
Spin, spin, ye mortals, I can smile,
Remembering this primeval plan
Watching with steady gaze meanwhile
The silent Oriental man.

THE MEN OF THE SHOVEL AND PICK.

THE last tie was laid on the highway of steel
    And fastened the last shining rail ;
The long parallels stretched away to the west
    On a road-bed of gravel and shale ;
And round by a curve was an onlooking crowd,
    Where an arm was uplifted to strike,
While glistened below in the sun's dying rays,
    The head of a solid gold spike.

There was sparkle of wine as they drove the
       spike home
    And eloquence thrilling to feel ;
The hand-clasp of continents almost it seemed
    This masculine gripping of steel ;
But over it all swept a whirling of wraiths
    As of snow-flakes foregathering thick,
Dim forms of forgotten ones, brawny, un-
      couth,
    The men of the shovel and pick.

Red-shirted, shag-bearded, and hairy of chest
  As Hercules rugged and strong,
They loomed like the heroes tense-muscled
    and stark
  That up from Mythology throng,
And all else faded out as the mist does at dawn
  While the clouds lifted, fold upon fold,
And tinged by the sunset, and framed in its
    rays
  A vision of battle unrolled.

For I saw a wide desert of alkali gray
  Where the dews never gladdened the plain,
Where no plant save the cactus uplifted its
    leaves
  And no drop ever fell of the rain ;
Yet here were these men in the pitiless sun,
  In the stifling and dust-laden air,
With their shovels and picks that were bran-
    dished on high
  By knotted arms, sunburned and bare.

And I saw them again in the cold autumn rain
  When the merciless desert was passed,
Saw them face the sharp sleet and enveloping
    snows
  In the storm-wake down-following fast ;

But they faltered not, failed not, nor looked
    they behind
  As those who grow weary and sore,
For each man was a knight and the weapons
    he had
  Were the shovel and pick that he bore.

And I saw them once more, when their eyes
    had beheld
  The Pacific's blue density roll,
And their lips were unclosed with the eagerness
    then
  Of a runner who bends to the goal ;
And from out of the ages an echo uprose
  Far-reaching and drifted to me,
A shout from the dust, call it dust if you will,
  Of " Thalassa, Thalassa, the sea ! !"

So I give not a thought to the spike of pure
    gold
  That finished the highway of steel,
Since the noblest is highest, not metal but men,
  And stamped with humanity's seal ;
And larger they loom, and still faster they come
  As the snow-flakes foregathering thick,
While I feel as I gaze that the last shall be first,
  These men of the shovel and pick.

ECCE SIGNUM.

THE wealth of Crœsus one had gained,
   One told his ancient line ;
Another honors high attained —
   They died, and made no sign.

One yielded life his friend to save,
   A beggar one did dine ;
One sang a song to free the slave —
   They died, but made the sign.

Oh, thou whose memory is the cross,
   And crown of thorns divine ;
Dear Christ, let me not know that loss
   To die, and make no sign.

THE BAR SINISTER.

THERE was a cruel king in olden times
Long, long ago, and like a subtle web,
His castle lay with drawbridge and with moat,
Portcullises, and sombre donjon keep;
And he, like some mailed spider, kept aloof
Till strangers came, wayfarers passing by,
And then he lured them to his inner halls
And kept them close in stern captivity.

So once there came a knight of goodly port
A youthful knight, and singing as he rode,
And past the gloomy castle would have spurred,
Had not the king, Ah! cunning were his ways,
Sent forth a seneschal in armor dressed
Of inlaid gold, who bade the knight to pause,
Until the message from the castle gates
Had been delivered and an answer given.

119

And thus began the wily seneschal
" My king doth send his greeting, and he says,
" That so ye come within his castle walls
" And enter in his service, so ye shall
" Be leader of his knights, and glory reap
" Such as no leader yet of high renown,
" Hath ever topp'd ; not Lion-Heart himself,
" The black-faced Richard, shall be peer of
    thine."

And said the listening knight with mien un-
    moved
" I enter not within thy liege's walls."

Then back returned the stately seneschal
And after him came out a wrinkled sage,
Some dark magician of those feudal days —
And heaped were both his palms with jewels
    rare,
Lone diamonds that held the steely flash
Of winter moonlight on a naked sword,
Emeralds as green as dense, unsounded seas,
And redder than the stain of roses bruised
Yea ! ruddier than January's sun,
Rubies he held, and sapphires too were there
That paled and gleamed alternate to the sight.

And quoth the ancient one, " Behold I bring
" All these and more, with countless hoards of
    gold
" For thee intact, an thou wilt come with me
" To serve my king, who waits thy gracious
    word."

And said the listening knight in cold disdain
" I enter not within thy liege's walls."

Then to the castle, lingering went the sage
While back returned to greet the waiting
    knight,
A woman of such presence that she seemed
Akin to that famed Helen of the Greeks,
Whom nations battled for in days agone ;
For tall was she, and graceful as an elm
And robed in white, with lilies at her throat,
Wind-blown her hair, that like a torrent fell
Full to her feet, a cataract of bronze ;
And in her eyes the lights and shadows
    changed
Of languor and of quick intelligence,
While every feature was all womanly
And beautiful beyond perfection's charm.

Her arms were bare, and smooth as ivory
While at her side she placed a silver harp,
And over all its strings her fingers ran
As light as thought, and following music came
Like running water, blent with plaintive winds;
And sweet it was, and powerful and strange,
As when one rises from a bed of boughs,
And stands at midnight under solemn stars
Listening alone, and hears the breezes thrill
With nameless chords the silence of the trees;
And when she sang the passion of her voice
Rang clear and high, then melted into tears.

And thus she gave her message to the knight
" If in thy gramercy thou seest fit
" To serve my liege, my father, and our land
" Lo ! I am thine, and king thou 'lt be in time
" With all the store of treasure promised thee,
" And high renown, as said the seneschal ;
" Wealth, glory, love, all, all is offered thee."

And said the listening knight with scornful
    smile
" I enter not within thy liege's walls."

And slowly back, the princess castlewards
Her steps retraced, and brought his answer
there ;
Whereat the king's grim forehead wrinkled
deep
The while he gave the mandate " Let him
pass."

But at the dawn, the curious seneschal
Upon the highway where the knight had
paused,
Did early search, and where the cavalier
Had made dismount to tighten saddle girths,
He found a sign that blanched his swarthy
cheek,
The print of cloven hoofs upon the sands.

THE PRODIGALS.

WHEN the roses of summer were budding and
    blooming
  And the yellow wheat bent 'neath its burden
    of gold,
The Prodigal Son came, world-weary and
    tattered,
  To the home where his footsteps had echoed
    of old.

And they clung to his garments with tears and
    caresses,
  Till the cup of his welcome ran over with
    joy,
And the flowers of love and forgiveness were
    woven
  In a blossoming crown for the Prodigal
    Boy.

When the icicles hung from the eaves and the
    branches,
    And the winter winds moaned round the
        dwellings of men,
Forsaken and homeless, the Prodigal Daughter
    Crept back to the home of her girlhood
        again.

But they turned her away in the storm and
    the darkness
    To the icy-cold winds with their ´chill,
        piercing breath,
And the pitiless curses that followed her
    footsteps
    Were fierce as the tempest and cruel as
        death !

DEAR HEART, SWEET HEART.

DEAR heart, sweet heart, your baby hands
    Have touched and passed this floating world,
Have loosed their hold on life's frail strands
    And now upon your breast lie furled
Twin blossoms of eternal peace,
    Like lilies on untroubled streams,
When the rude winds have made surcease
    And summer's glory drifts and dreams.

Dear heart, sweet heart, your waxen lips
    Shall never touch my cheek again,
For they are steeped in an eclipse
    Which lies beyond my mortal ken ;
And that great sphinx of death who keeps
    ` His silent vigil over all,
Has left your face as one who sleeps —
    Save for the bosom's rise and fall.

Dear heart, sweet heart, your tender eyes
    With all their depths of wondering,
Are closed for aye ; as droops and dies
    The first sweet violet bank of spring ;
And their far look of thought unthought
    Shall never come again, or be,
Since this remorseless change was wrought,
    That closed the gates 'twixt thee and me.

Dear heart, sweet heart, the lonely way
    Seems doubly steep since you are gone,
The dawn has faded out of day,
    The rose has faded out of dawn ;
And I, alas, must needs go down
    My hand unclasped by any child,
To wear the Cross without the crown
    And walk through life unreconciled.

Dear heart, sweet heart, 'mid hopes and fears
    I bend and kiss you, thus, and thus ;
Mine eyes are dim with brimming tears
    My lips with grief are tremulous ;
My baby boy — that you should die
    And out into the darkness go,
Beyond my broken-hearted cry,
    I loved you so, I loved you so.

THE CHRISTIAN.

THERE was a tawny woman of the sands
Lithe-limbed and rounded, and who moved at
     ease
With sinuous grace as some wild leopardess
On desert wilds ; and black her piercing eyes
As the great vulture's of the snowy peaks,
Who all day long hung pendent in the clouds
And watched the lazy caravans pace by.

And whiles there came a traveller in those
     ways
And sat him down beside the desert well,
Ate the dry dates and cooled his parching lips
And told strange tales of a mysterious God
Who ruled the world, and taught the willing
     stars,
To whirl submissive in their orbits round ;
And sang his praises with inspiring voice
Till in the breast of this lone creature leaped
A pulsing flame of hope that flickered up
As dawn's faint tapers light unwilling skies.

Over her troubled fancy then there came
A vague outreaching of awakened life,
And filled with helpful longing for her kind,
She left the green oasis of her youth
And traversed many a mile of burning sands,
Until the gates of pagan cities loomed
Before her pathway menacing and bare.

And entering in, with rapt, transfigured face,
She spent her days and sacrificed her nights
Until at length, the pagan language learned,
With eager lips she told the Christian creed,
The love of God, the spotless life of Christ,
Faith, hope, and charity, and tenderness.

And when the pagans made a holiday
They gave her to the lions for her pains.

AS FOR ME, I HAVE A FRIEND.

LET the sower scatter seed
  Where the crumbling furrows blend ;
Let the churchman praise his creed
  The beginning and the end ;
  As for me, I have a friend.

Does the sun forget to shine
  And the wind blow sere and chill ?
Does the cluster leave the vine,
  And the ice begird the rill ?
  I shall rest contented still.

Must the rose be stripped of leaf
  When the waning June has passed ?
Shall an autumn voice its grief
  In the lorn November blast ?
  What of that, a friend will last.

Why should I, then, make complaint
   To the days that round me roll?
She my' missal is, and saint,
   Clad in womanhood's white stole,
   She, the keeper of my soul.

Not love's chalice to my lips,
   Not that bitter draught she brings,
Which as Hybla's honey drips
   And like bosomed asp-worm stings,
   No! she tells of happier things.

Simple friendship, just that much
   To enfold me as a strand
Of her hair might; and the touch
   Of a gracious, welcoming hand
   That I grasp, and understand.

Let death ope or lock his gate
   Let the lilies break or bend,
And the iron will of fate
   Sorrows now or fortune send,
   As for me, I have a friend.

IN PASSING.

THROUGH halls whose carven panels held
    A host of cherubim,
Up stairways wide I wandered on
    Through curtained vistas dim,
And ever as my footsteps came
    By alcove, hall and stair,
A myriad mirrors started up
    And caught my shadow there.

Sometimes my profile paled and sank
    A smile upon my lips.
Sometimes a blur my features were
    Swift darkening to eclipse ;
But following as these figures fled
    Faint ghosts of grayish gleams —
I walked beside, as one who walks
    Companioned in his dreams.

132

Oh ! winding years that round my path
  Like mirrors flash and pass,
Once, always, do you hold for me
  The wraith within the glass ;
Some night or day, some star or sun
  (As what should say, " Beware !")
Reveals in your dead seasons' flight
  My shadow passing there.

FOAM-WRAITHS AND DRIFTWOOD.

THE SEA.

LIKE some lone, wild creature that paces all
  day,
  Back and forth behind bars in its dumb,
   strong wish to be free,
So paces forever all haggard and gray,
  On its earth-bound shores, the mysterious
   soul of the sea.

All through the night, when silvery moon and
  stars
  Gleam from their heights above, on the
   restless waters below,
And all day long, still beating against its bars,
  Surges the might of the Ocean in endless
   ebb and flow.

Ebb and flow, in a mournful ceaseless pacing,
  Shaking its barriers firm, with tireless,
   tremulous hands,
And its steps in sadness tracing and slowly
  retracing
  On prison floors of pallid and shifting sands.

137

DERELICT.

UNHEEDED from the main-top mast
    Her fluttering pennon sweeps ;
The anchor from the cat-head hangs
    No hand the tiller keeps ;
No sailors man her creaking yards
    No storms her ways restrict,
As on through wastes of billowy seas
    She wanders, derelict.

Her skipper is old Boreas
    Her master is the sea ;
No shout across the plunging waves
    May reach to such as she ;
And woe to that unhappy wretch
    Who signals her to save,
For she is naught but passionless
    And passive as the grave.

138

For her the vast and briny deep
  That still unceasing rolls,
The veering change of time and tide
  The tropics, and the poles ;
What recks she now of welcoming port
  Or voyage yet to be ?
What boots the cry of " Ship ahoy "
  To vagrants of the sea ?

Alike to her the seasons pass
  With sunlight or with snow,
Alike to her are dusk and dawn,
  And refluent ebb and flow,
Of rain or shine she recketh not
  Nor scent of pine or palm,
And one to her the miracles
  Of hurricane and calm.

No hope is centred in her fate
  No souls upon her sail,
Companioned only by the winds
  That through her rigging trail,
For her no hands are clasped in prayer
  Nor anxious eyes bedimmed,
As black against the moon's bright disc
  Her sombre spars are limned.

But light and shade shall still be hers
   The white wake off to lee —
Pale starlight, and a myriad stars
   Night-etched upon the sea,
And in her shrouds the wind will sing
   And sea-birds round her play,
As dumbly on her questless quest
   She follows day by day.

And they who for her cargo seek
   Will track the seas in vain;
Will plough the wave, but never reap,
   A harvest from the main;
For her tall masts the lookout keen
   In vain the skies will scan,
Abandoned — she shall know no more
   The tyranny of man.

But with the wind and wave and foam
   In freedom will she toss,
And spread her canvas to the breeze
   As some great albatross;
And proudly shall her dark prow dip
   As courtiers bend the knee
To greet their sovereign, as she greets,
   Her sovereign lord, the sea.

And thus a wraith, a mote, a speck,
    In watery solitudes,
She sails, and hears the siren song
    Of ocean's circe-moods ;
For neither home nor harbor bound
    Naught shall her course restrict,
While, like men's souls in worlds to come
    She wanders, derelict.

AN ETCHING.

I STOOD upon a stretch of sandy shore,
Around me hung the shadows of the night,
The rising tide came creeping o'er the beach.

Far out along the mighty ocean fell
The garments of the dusk, fold after fold,
And through the ebon barriers on high
The stars looked down upon a sleeping world ;
Fresh from the waves a rich sea-incense came
Salt-sweet and pure, and drifted idly past,
To wander in the midst of distant woods,
Where violets and sweet wood-flowers grew.

Then from the darkling seas the moon rose up,
Up from unsounded depths and lay across
The black expanse of waters like a shield ;
And suddenly upon its pallid sheen
A ship was etched, in clear-cut, stately lines,
And seemed to hang, a picture in the sky.

With sails all spread, with pennant far out-
     stretched,
Spars, masts and rigging, all in form exact,
Held for a moment in a silver disc
Etched by the wayward touch of flitting
     chance.
So for an instant did I see it thus
And then it vanished, quickly as a dream,
Dropped from its shining frame to nothingness
From shadows born to shadow-land returned.

So men are etched upon the glass of fate ;
So gleams and vanishes the ship of life.

.

DROWNED.

FAR in the folds of the pitiless deeps
  Where dense blue waters in silence go
Back and forth as the tide-wave sweeps
  In the dusky vaults of the sea below,
With his hair blown out in streaming strands
  And the film of death on his strange set eyes,
A bit of plank in his tight-clenched hands,
  A sailor stretched in his slumber lies.

Never a prayer or a burial hymn
  For one whose grave is the restless deep,
Where waves roll on through the arches dim
  And shadows over the billows creep
Back and forth in a ceaseless race,
  As ebbs and flows the wandering tide,
The pallid stare of a fixed, white face,
  And nerveless arms that are flung aside.

144

And never a sound can reach him there
    From the blue sea's breast or its outmost rim,
A sweetheart's cry or a mother's prayer
    Never can touch or awaken him ;   .
And Gabriel's trump on the last dark day,
    Will call in vain from its briny bed,
The sailor's soul, for it rests for aye
    With the uncalled souls mid the Ocean's
        dead.

THE MERMAID'S SONG.

In ocean reefs my home lies hid,
   And dark sea shadows o'er me
Wind in and out the waves amid
   Or stand in gloom before me :
Till, drifting down upon the deep
   Comes day, a message bringing
That wakes the billows from their sleep
   And sets the shells to singing.

I know the inner haunts of caves
   That line the rocky reaches,
I know the secrets of the waves
   That break on lonely beaches ;
I hear the waters come and go
   As far the ocean ranges,
And listen to the ebb and flow
   That mark the pale moon's changes.

146

For me the rocks where sea-weed clings
    Like winding wreaths of laurel,
Where spectral music rolls and rings
    Through shining groves of coral,
For me the spell of weaving hands
    For me the meadows vernal,
Where mermaids dance in mystic bands
    To ocean's chant eternal.

FALSE CHORDS.

I LISTEN, but I listen all in vain,
Amid the jangle of be-ribboned lyres
(The which our modern poets strum upon.)
For some heart-note, some echo of great
    thoughts
To thrill me and uplift me like the breath
Of sudden brine from out old ocean's breast,
Fresh-dashing in my face a kiss of dawn.

But so it is, that all I hear — good God,
Is art, art, art, and sickly plaintive runes
Of flowers, birds, and lovelorn serenades,
In cunning form, fine moulded for the ear,
Frail word-mosaics of these lesser days ;
Or failing that, there comes a mystic chant
Of dense, dull verse, whose secret lies in
    gloom,
Swathed like a mummy in his cerements.

And these are nothing but false chords, I
    know ;
For true-born singers smite Apollo's harp
With something of the spirit of a god,
And give their very life-blood to the song.

Oh, muse of mine, let not my lyre sound
To such vain pipings ; grant its varied moods
A touch of tears — a voice of nature's own
As lucid, and as free and undefiled ;
And give it steel, and iron, like the strength
Of clashing sabres and of bayonets
And black-mouthed cannon, wreathed in thun-
    der clouds,
Whose music rolls a menace o'er the skies
Where earth is shaking to the tread of Mars.

THE SEVENTH DAUGHTER.

THE seventh daughter paced the shore
    Nor star nor moon was there in heaven,
But boom of breakers and the roar
    Of thunder, and the lightning's levin,
The sea leaped up and landward bore
    And she was last was born of seven.

The dank grass bent beneath the blast
    And far and near were whitecaps flying,
And storm-blown sea-birds as they passed
    Discordant through the night were crying,
And on the reefs with broken mast
    A shattered ship, broached-to, was lying.

Now bring the spell of weaving hands
    Of weaving hands and woven paces,
Of magic, and air-plaited strands
    Of wimpled locks round elvish faces,
While down along the dripping sands
    The white-maned surf-host romps and races.

A rocket lights the sullen skies
   With one red flash of flame-elation,   '
And slowly o'er the billows dies
   A cannon's dull reverberation,
With never ending fall and rise
   Of wave on wave in swift rotation.

They lash the women to the spars
   The rough reef grinds, the good ship lunges,
Above the bars and round the bars
   The ocean gathers, rises, plunges,
And through the crushed and splintered scars
   The green brine soaks as into sponges.

Go get you gone of seventh birth
   Your arts and spells no respite gave them,
Nor prayers indeed were aught of worth
   Since that the deep-sea forces crave them,
And naught of all that rests on earth
   Or sits above has power to save them.

The seventh daughter paced the shore
   The dawn had come, the storm was riven,
Six sisters had she now no more
   Six souls had passed to hell or heaven,
The sea was level as a floor
   And she was last was born of seven.

WHITE CAPS.

Over the cool green wall of waves advancing
  Glistens a crested line of feathery foam,
Till along the beach the billows scatter, glanc-
    ing
  A mist of spray as over the waters comb ;
Then fades the white-capped crest all slowly
    sinking
Where silent, shadowy sands are ever drinking,
    drinking.

Into the sunlight's gleam a gray gull flashes
  Into the salt-sea air on buoyant wing,
High above where the prisoned sea incessant
    dashes —
  Poises just for an instant, wavering,
Veers to the right, and then its vague flight
    shifting,
Falls to the waves, and with the waves goes
    drifting, drifting.

Over the sea, miles out, a ship is riding,
   Threading the ocean paths with oaken keel,
And under her bow the baffled waves are
     sliding
   As over her sails the rising breezes steal,
And in her wake a foamy track is lying
As northward far she sails still flying, flying.

And in my heart and soul a voice is ringing
   Like Circe's voice, and saying unto me,
I am a voice immortal ever singing
   The glory and the sorrow of the sea ;
Whose waves like human feet press on forever,
Whose soul like human souls is happy never,
     never.

THE FLYING DUTCHMAN.

WHERE the tide crept up in a stealthy way
By the reefs and hollows of Table Bay,
The dwellings rude of the Dutchmen lay.

And the night approached with a sign of storm
For the winds blew cold and the winds blew
    warm,
And cloud-rack high in the skies would form.

And far to the right in the lone cape's lee
A vessel surged in the wallowing sea,
And the white-caps gleamed and the winds rose
    free.

'T was the brig that carried the Holland mails
Through the summer's calm or the winter gales
And her pennant streamed o'er her tawny sails.

A giant she was in a giant's grip
For the dark seas clung to the struggling ship
And the salt brine down from the shrouds did
    drip.

And her sails were wet with the glancing spray,
As she rose through the gathering darkness
    gray,
And her bow was headed for Table Bay.

But the sea beat back with a sodden force
The Dutchman's ship in its wandering course,
And the thunder's mockery bellowed hoarse.

And a woman waited beside a tree
In the moan of the winds and the branches
    dree,
For a letter to come that night by sea.

Then shouted the mate to the skipper there
"Turn back," so sounded his trumpet's blare,
"Or our seams will split and our masts stand
    bare."

But Vanderdecken drew his blade
And the steely sheen that its flashing made
Struck light from the all-surrounding shade,

And his anger stood in his bristling hair,
While his furious sword-stroke smote the air,
As he stood alone in defiance there.

And he swore to weather the stubborn gale
With its rattling volleys of icy hail,
If it stripped from the masts each tattered sail.

And to beat around for that very bay,
And where was the one who could say him
    nay —
" By God ! if he sailed till the judgment day."

Then the mist grew dense and the lightning
    flashed
And a red bolt down on the tree-top crashed
Where a woman stood by the shore, sea-lashed.

And the thunder tolled in the blackening clouds
And the waves swept by in hurrying crowds,
And a wan light paled in the creaking shrouds.

While a scream came by from the far-off shore,
That was hushed and drowned by the mad
    waves' roar,
And the vessel passed and was seen no more.

And now on that self-same fateful night
If the seas be calm and the skies are bright,
The ocean giveth a mystic sight.

For a shadow-ship in a shadow-frame
Looms out at twelve through the moonlight's
    flame
Passing as suddenly as it came.

And a whisper thrills through the salt-sweet
    breeze,
While a heart-throb stirs in the moving seas,
And the tide fast out to the ocean flees.

And a fine wind stirs in the tree-top high
That ghostly stands in the starlit sky,
And a sound wells up like a woman's sigh.

But when on that night the clouds turn black
And the huge waves follow the storm-king's
    track
And the skies are heavy with tempest-wrack,

Why then is seen, as a spectre gray
Mid the shimmering mist and lightning-play
A vessel headed for Table Bay.

And the ship, like a lover, keeps her troth
To her skipper's pledge — 't was a pledge for
    both —
And the wild winds echo the Dutchman's oath,

And a wraith waits there by the haunted tree
While the storm wails on, and the wind blows
    free,
For a letter which comes not in from sea.

157

COLOMBO.

ONE day in August, fourteen ninety-two,
So long ago in an old port of Spain,
Where reared the skies an arc of deepest blue
And summer's glories had begun to wane,
In Ferdinand and Isabella's reign
Three ships sailed out upon a fateful quest,
Borne far across upon a watery plain
By blandest winds against their rigging pressed,
The creaking spars outspread, and prows
    toward the west.

And Palos in the distance faded out
The moss-grown quay, the grayish olive trees,
And changing groups that slowly moved about
Seen dimly o'er the track of sprayey seas,
While churches, masts, and towers, even these
At length were gone and only echoing bells
Borne faintly on the pinions of the breeze,
Came stealing softly o'er the heaving swells
And fell upon their hearts like sound of ghostly
    knells.

And all before was a lone waste immense
Far seas unsounded and as yet unsailed,
And shrouded in a mystery as dense
As fabled Isis in her temple veiled,
Yet fared they forth by storm and wave assailed
While stretched the glistening canvas as they
    passed,
And up aloft the listless pennants trailed,
When dreamy calm the deep green waters
    glassed
And white, still clouds above in the clear
    heavens massed.

Gone was the sailor's song and cheery smile
As steadily they drifted day by day,
For journeying on, each home-dividing mile·
Seemed as a hand that put them far away ;
For superstition held them in its sway ;
And ignorance, and passion, but the man·
Whose granite will was mightier than they·
Still held his carved, black bowsprit in the van.
And under stars and sun the restless surge
    would scan.

For he was oak and iron, and he stood
Among them like a lion while his air
Had all the stern, unbending hardihood
Of those who have done battle with despair ;

Long had he known of penury and care,
Neglect and disappointment and disdain
Yet kept the courage that could do and dare,
And dauntless here through tempest, wind and
    rain
Bore westward with his sullen crews across
    the main.

And as they sailed sharp cloud peaks were un-
    furled
In airy space where swam the dying sun,
And seemed reflections of their promised world
As rose the flame tipped summits, one by one,
And then would fall the twilight's mantle dun
With twinkling stars and weirdest moonlight
    glow,
Where broken clouds along the skies would
    run
And night-winds through the straining ropes
    would blow
While lapped and lapped again the waters far
    below.

And gleamed the myriad foam-streaks in their
    wake
Pale, feathery spume, by wandering sea-birds
    crossed,

That melted as would melt a fragile flake,
Of winter snows when in an eddy tossed,
And sometimes level seas by sunlight glossed
Basked idly where the idle vessels lay
Within an ocean-desert's vagueness lost,
While westward still stood out the vasty gray
That changed not, save for weary change of
  night and day.

· But on a sudden instant to their sight
The western world, a mystery no more,
In emerald tints of freshest verdure bright
Rose through the mist, the long, long-looked
    for shore ;
Past the hoarse tumult of the breakers' roar
Where tufted palms shot upward from the grass
Casting their shade the shell-strewn beaches
    o'er
While glittered fiery sands like burnished brass,
With swinging flowery vines by pool and dank
    morass.

I sing the gallant spirit of the man
Colombo, he of Genoa, who drave
His carved and blackened bowsprit in the van
Of that wild journey o'er the trackless wave,

To find a continent or fill a grave,
Under the shadows of the western skies ;
Who all his years to one grand purpose gave,
And looking out from his high soul's surmise
Saw with a prophet's gaze though through a
    dreamer's eyes.

POLPERRO.

Polperro — it lies where the Cornish Cliffs
   whiten
  Sheer heights that flash up in the light of
     the sun,
And below each grave peak that looms huge
     as a Titan
  The tides and the tidal sweep shimmering
     run,
The tides and the tidal sweep, green, briny
     water
  That pours over sands where the singing
     shells be,
The gray, pallid sands that turn hotter and
     hotter
  In the grasp of the sun by the shores of
     the sea.

Oh! sun, there are depths where thy lambent
     rays never
  Strike, quiver or bask over lustreless sands,

Where the light and the shade shall not meet,
    shall not sever
  As the yearning of hearts or unclasping of
    hands ;
Where the gulf-stream glides onward through
    emerald crystal
  And ripple there is none to ruffle the
    deep,
Where not even the wail of the storm-laden
    mistral
  Disturbs the repose of the waters that
    sleep.

And forever and ever the lone sail shall
    glisten
  And forever the fishers go down to the
    sea,
And the drear nights shall come when the
    fisher-wives listen
  (The light on the sill and the wind in the
    tree.)
The light on the sill and the stars in the hazes
  That leadenly drift in the lowering skies,
While the salt spray that beats on each pale
    face that gazes
  Sharp, stingingly sharp through the wind-
    spaces flies.

And or ever or never the fisher finds haven
    And the tear will be dried by the kiss on
        the lips,
The ripe, ruddy lips where the prayer-words
        were graven
    In the darkness and storm for the weather-
        worn ships ;
And a child will croon low where a south
        wind shall blow you
    A sweet breath of daisies from far inland lea,
And a long shred of sunlight shall smilingly
        throw you
    A kiss from the sea.

HAUD A WEE MY WILLIE.

LIGHT o' heart and careless hand
Siller nane nor yet o' land
Save the wee bit beach o' sand
    Haud a wee my Willie.

Wha shall tak' his empty seat
In the life-boat, thro' the weet,
When the ragin' billows beat,
    Haud a wee my Willie.

Never he did danger shirk
Light o' day or glow'rin' mirk,
Bared his breast to face the work,
    Haud a wee my Willie.
        ,

Foremost hand to launch the boat
Knotted kerchief at his throat,
Whis'lin' like the plover's note,
    Haud a wee my Willie.
        166

Fathoms deep he's lyin' now
Sea-weed matted on his brow,
Where the winds the waters plough,
    Haud a wee my Willie.

Nane to heed o' joy or bliss
Nane to ken nor yet to miss,
Mither's warnin' — sweetheart's kiss,
    Haud a wee my Willie.

OFF PELICAN POINT.

STRAIGHT out from the rocky headland,
   I swim in the soft moonshine,
The air is heavy with shadows
   The shadows are drenched in brine,
And the salt-sweet savor and flavor
   Thrills keen through my veins like wine.

The chant of the shoreward breakers
   Beats up to the cliffs above,
As restless in rhyme and rhythm
   As the tide it whispers of,
And the sea-weed folds me and holds me
   Like the arms of her I love.

The stark waves break at my shoulder
   The spray is tart on my lips,
A long swell looms in the foreground
   Then back to the rearward slips,
And the echoings hollow follow
   Where the great sea rolls and dips.

Low plaints of the pulsing water
   Faint chords from the under sea,
Cool winds through the strands of starlight
   That glitter away to lee,
And the twilight ringing and singing
   Are the sounds that come to me.

The track of the floating moonlight
   Half beckoning lures me on,
As though it led to the harbor
   Where the home-bound souls have gone,
And its ghostly glimmer and shimmer
   As a dead man's face is wan.

I lie on the sad sea's bosom
   Or with swift stroke cleaving pass,
Where foam-crests tipped by the star-shine
   Stand high in a fluffy mass,
And the billows down under sunder
   Over depths as green as glass.

With stars in the skies to lend me
   Far glints from a world divine,
I toss as a careless swimmer
   And the deep-sea joys are mine,
Forgetting to borrow sorrow
   Throat-deep in the buoyant brine.

The boom of the surf behind me
    And the crag's sharp lines above,
Fade out and in God's wide heaven
    Peace broods as a nesting dove,
And the waters fold me and hold me
    Like the arms of her I love.

OFF GEORGES BANKS.

Off Georges Banks the sun went down
  In crimson splendor gleaming,
As past the bar a vessel sailed
  With graceful pennant streaming ;
And in her wake across the blue
A stormy petrel flew.

Then from their ambush crept the winds
  To wake each sleeping billow ;
And in their grasp the strong masts shook
  Like slender twigs of willow,
And struck by whips of foaming spray
The good ship bore away.

Through darkling clouds the lightning clove
  A jagged path asunder ;
And in the gloomy vaults o'erhead
  Deep rolled the sullen thunder ;
While high above unnumbered graves
Up leaped the hungry waves.

Gray rose the dawn ; and dreamily,
   As though 'twixt sleep and waking ;
Low lapped the waves, as on the rocks
   Their long, green lines were breaking ;
And in the changing sky afar,
Paled out a single star.

Then seaward from the lonely reefs
   The sun came up all slowly,
His first beams touched a white, white face,
   Among the seaweed lowly,
A dead face lashed to floating planks
Drowned there — off Georges Banks.

ADRIFT.

A FRAIL, rude raft, wave-tossed on midnight
    seas ;
  Three shadow-spars across the moon's gold
    glow —
A ragged shape that rose from bended knees
And cried " Sail ho ! "

THE NORTHWEST PASSAGE.

I.

WHERE Arctic currents curl and flash
   And death prowls over wastes of snow,
Where giant icebergs sway and crash
   Into the chilling depths below,
The Northwest passage spectral stands
And beckons men to Polar lands.

II.

A ruined hut, an empty chest ;
   A blackened remnant of a sail ; —
A tattered record tells the rest
   While northern winds in dirges wail ;
And from the icebergs cold tears drip
Upon a crushed and rotting ship.

A BOTTLE.

I.

In a cabin locker for many a year
    A bottle lay ;
And whether the weather was fair and clear
    Or whether the Ocean was rough and gray,
The bottle had nothing to care or fear ;
    Yet the ship was an iron oaken mass
    And the other was nothing but brittle glass —
        A bottle.

II.

Where the billows rose highest the storm-king
        flew
    Over the sea ;
And the waters foamed and the wild winds
        blew,   .
    While the mad waves tossed in a whirling
        glee,
And all that was left of a ship and crew
    Came, bringing its message with silent lips
    Of the perils of those who go down in ships —
        A bottle.

MY CHAPTER.

THE BURNING OF THE SHIPS.

I.

WHERE pillars stood with roses garlanded
And rhythmic music, rising, rose and fell,
And many faces turned enquiring gaze
A man and woman met.
                 Like ship to ship
That crash together and recoil and drift
In watery wastes and darkness, so their souls
Felt the rebound ; and lifting up their eyes
O'ershadowed like a hand with wonderment,
Each looked across, and in their thoughts arose
The inward spoken question, " Who art thou ?"

Then hand met hand and evermore the sense
Grew, as a rose of that companionship
Which flaunts the petal while it hides the thorn ;
For fate, which found them in that one first
      glance,
Held them apart, and, like the Barmecide
Brought nothing and yet bade them eat and
      drink ;
And heart to heart came following afterwards
As bud will follow blossom.

This is true —
Each man and woman has a counterpart,
A twin-born soul which wanders up and down
Seeking its mate ; and whether such have been
As comrades in another world than this,
I know not ; ask the Sibyl, but I know
These two were for each other.

So days went by to blend with starry nights
And midnights paled and trembled into dawn,
And gathering fast with still intensity
As snows come crowding to an avalanche,
So all their hopes came silently and sure
To touch, and cross, and mingle, and be one.

There may be much in silence ; most of all
The silence of strong natures ; as an oak
Half century old will breathless stand and wait
Through listless summer days, nor move a leaf
Until the storm awakes it, when it flings
Rough branches to the winds and every root
And limb and fibre quivers in the gale.

So was it with these two.   No word of love
Had left their lips, and comrades they had
    seemed
By many a stretch of sombre woods and sere,

By many a mile of wave-encircled sands,
By many a field of swallow-haunted grass ;
And they had walked the city streets and ways
And made no sign, and heard no warning voice.

II.

There was a night, I think a night of nights,
Dim lit with little stars, there was no moon,
Wild winds across the darkness, and a note
Of Neptune's horn beside the lonely sea ;
And these twain passed together, and the flight
Of breezes riotous and whirling leaves
Went northward high above them, and a glint
Of cloudy starlight flecked the distant sky.

And somewhere in the lapses of the storm,
Somewhere within the hollows of the dusk
A sudden silence blossomed, and these two
Solving the riddle of their lives at last
Turned, with a wordless message on the lips,
And like to those who have been parted long
Clung fast to one another and were glad.

There was no speech nor promises nor tears
But soul to soul their higher being met
As current meets with current where a stream
Gains in its height and steadily flows on.

Nor was there doubt nor lesser sense of fear,
And star by star the constellations came
To sleep along the waters ; and the leaves,
The dry, dead leaves that lay across their path
Rustled and stirred, and overhead the trees
Made mighty moan because it came to pass.

And yet, and yet if custom had her say
Or sterner still that harsh dame Precedent,
Doubt not these two did wrongly ; for the world
Sees, spectacled with envy and distrust,
And ever looking downward ;

                         But indeed,
Love's light keeps bright the windows of the
    soul
And these knew neither evil nor dismay,
Because, forsooth, a law ruled so and so
A custom this, a principle thus much,
But simply said, "Thy hand and mine inwove
There is not that which comes 'twixt me and
    thee."

I question not of usage nor of creed,
And care not, lacking that subservience
Which doffs the hat to mediocrity
And worships still the outward shell of things ;

For there are times and trials when the mind
Can reckon not by means of rule and rote,
But with its present doubts enstranded round
Must cut the gordian knot and doubt no more.

And so they made their compact and were wise,
And burned the ships behind them as they
        passed
Like those old hardy Norsemen when they
        came
To shores unconquered, and thus new and
        strange.

And hand in hand they wandered on and on
And heart with heart they vanished from my
        sight,
And soul to soul I doubt not now they stand
Upon the heights that further inland lie,
Those happier heights, free-stretching and
        remote
Where bloom the lilies of the dawn and shine
Midsummer suns on grassy slopes and green.

MY LADY OF LILIES.

SHE with her serious moods, and her moods
  fantastic,
   Whimsical, various, sad and glad, a woman,
     in just a word,
Now with a tender tone and again with a tone
  sarcastic
   By passion and impulse swayed as the deep
     sea depths are stirred,
But I love her, and under her touch my soul
  grows plastic
   And just to think of her stills my heart and
     my eyes are blurred.

For God's best work after all at the best was
  woman
   Judge her and test her and note her faults,
     no doubt you can,
But indeed, as the world's page reads she is
  yet more human
   Loving and faithful and more forgiving than
     lesser man,

And ever since Adam the natures of men were
    common,
    Mere quartz, where as veined and virgin
      gold her finer nature ran.

Oh! Lady of Lilies, and mine by the one
    word spoken
    Mine when the gathering snowflakes fall or
      when roses bloom,
Mine by the fiat of fate and the silence broken
    Mine through the days, or nights that the
      northern lights illume,
I wear the thorns, I kiss the flowers, and
    accept the token
    And her face is the one bright thread in my
      life's dull loom.

The seasons come and they go with the dead
    leaves falling
    The springtide sinks in the summer, the
      blossom forsakes the bee,
And autumn comes with a purple wand the
    woods enthralling
    Till the winds from the north find harbor by
      the shores of a wintry sea,
But season and season and change on change
    one voice is calling
    And an echo catches it up and brings it back
      to me.

I go my way and the way is steep, the way is
    lonely
  But the breeze blows fresh and the long
    long miles can never tire,
And the erstwhile shadows that rose, in the
    dust are lying pronely
  While my hands are stretched to her in a
    keen, untold desire,
Oh ! Lady of mine, my own, whose love re-
    deems me only,
  Passionate, pure as the coldest star, and with
    heart of fire.

KISMET.

I TOSSED her picture on the coals
   Against the black-log glowing red,
And snaky flames, Medusa-like
   Coiled and uncoiled about her head,
And lo ! the insensate card-board lived
   The fire had set its spirit free,
And lovingly her fair white arms
   Rose up to clasp and cling to me.

And when the picture blackened lay,
   Upon its film a profile true,
Unrolled in hazy silhouette
   Then darted up the chimney's flue,
And where above the ashes gray
   A blue flame-bubble seemed to float,
I straightway saw her face again
   A bunch of violets at her throat.

Oh ! nevermore may I be freed
   From this her presence ; 't is too late.
" Bismillah ! " so the Moslem cries
   And I the Christian, echo " Fate ! "
I raze her image from my heart
   I put away her voice — and she —
Comes back to where our pathways met
   And walks the journey's end with me.

DE MI AMIGO.

FOR you the fig and olive shine
    The green leaf spreads and waters run,
With scarlet banners of the vine
    And gleam of lizard in the sun,
For me the leafless tree and black,
    The iron weight of winter's ire,
And some cold meteor's baleful track
    That sails beyond a wake of fire.

To you shall come the glint of seas
    Blue-dappled in the glance of dawn,
With threads of many a languid breeze
    Through warp and woof of leaf-looms
        drawn,
To me December's steely mail
    That armors all the lakes and streams,
And far-off skies that are as pale
    As some dead spring time's crocus gleams.

189

What ! will you tempt me with the thought
    Of living summer, I who stand
Where every sunbeam glistens taut
    Ice-girdled in this northern land ?
Nor leaf, nor bud, nor blossom's glow
    Hath 'scaped the storm king's icy clutch,
To lend above the barren snow
    Some hope or hint of April's touch.

Your phrase of soft Castilian sung
    Shall lull me not to dreamful sleep
The hammer-stroke of Saxon tongue
    Alone can pass the guard I keep;
The caballero's old guitar
    In southern clime sounds sweet and low,
But Hengist's song was aye for war —
    The bill, the axe, the bended bow.

I yield the charm of gentler speech
    For most melodious interlude,
Yet harsher accents still may teach
    A nobler meaning, grant it rude ;
For who that hears a bugle call
    Shall tell of music more divine ;
A Circe's voice, enchanting all,
    Made heroes level with the swine.

And for the light of tropic noon,
　　The shrill cicala in the grass,
The full, slow splendor of the moon,
　　Where nights like slippered shadows pass,
I send you word of frozen lanes
　　Where clear is etched the horseshoe dint,
And frost-lace on the window-panes
　　And fields as hard as mountain flint.

Yet for your friendship and its sign —
　　The message sent — I hold them dear
In sun and snow, in rain or shine,
　　Or whether skies be dark or clear,
And somewhere out from fancy sprung
　　I keep, though wide our paths apart
A Saxon word upon my tongue,
　　Its Spanish echo in my heart.

BY OUR AIN FIRESIDE.

'T is we twain, 't is we twain
By our ain fireside;
Adown the window glides the rain
The embers in the ashes hide,
'T is we twain, we twain,
By our ain fireside.

I know not why it seems to be
So much to watch the coals with thee,
So much to sit here hand in hand
Near smoke-wreath dim and smouldering brand
'T is we twain,
        By our ain fireside.

'T is we twain, 't is we twain
By our ain fireside ;
Swart shadows flit across the pane
And you and I in silence bide ;
'T is we twain, we twain,
By our ain fireside.

To-night this hearth-glow leaping thus
Shall make a merry jest for us,
For who so far apart as we?
And yet — repeat it after me,
'T is we twain,
        By our ain fireside.

'T is we twain, 't is we twain
By our ain fireside ;
I smile on you, and mocking feign
That you my sweetheart are or bride,
'T is we twain, we twain,
By our ain fireside.

IN A MISSOURI ORCHARD.

THIS is the path and this the tree
Whose blossoms drink the air of May,
And there the self-same meadowy sea
In undulations rolls away ;
And here an ancient granite stone
Is in the grasses sinking low,
No changes now to me are shown
Save that one haunting change alone —
I miss the face I used to know.

I see as through a mist of tears
The summer of a golden past,
And dark across the day appears
The shadow that old time has cast ;
Yet, hark ! the same blithe cricket sings
Down in the leaf-beds hiding low,
I hear the brush of passing wings
And sounds of once familiar things
But miss the voice I used to know.

The breeze upon the languorous air
Lifts the lithe branches one by one,
And I and silence, silent share
The glowing semi-southern sun,
I see the green Missouri hills
I feel the blossoms round me blow,
And all my heart with longing fills
As memory through my being thrills
A hand-clasp that I used to know.

The house upon the rise that sweeps
A curve of emerald to the west,
Is still the same, and dumbly keeps
Its place like some deserted nest.
Oh! hopes, that down the long days fled
Oh! blossoms with your hearts of snow,
Oh! death when all save me are dead,
Would fate had taken me instead,
And not the one I used to know.

A SANDAL-WOOD FAN.

The fan of silk and sandal-wood
That lay within her shapely hand,
Moved light as any cloud-film could
That idly sails o'er sea and land,
While some faint breath from foreign strand
Rose, languorous, as it curved and swayed,
Spiced scents of burning Samarcand
Telling of tropic sun and shade.

The roses at her supple throat
Were opening to their coming close
With those deep tinges which denote
The coloring of that reddest rose
The Jacqueminot — while still her fan,
That subtle, sensuous sandal-wood,
Had drugged me with its drowsy mood
Like poppy-juice of Turkestan.

Her lips, her eyes, her tawny hair,
Her dress of wavering velvet sheen
With its pale tints of olive-green,
Grew on me like a vision fair ;

And moved the fan as if it seemed
To lull me, as I lulling dreamed,
While all the air was heavy there
With drifting fumes of odorous spice
Which locked my senses in a vise.

The actor strutting on the stage
I saw no more — the mimic play
Had faded as a moonbeam may
Writ on a river's liquid page ;
I saw the face of Helen then,
I heard the voice of Circe sweep
Across a stilled, enchanted deep,
Enchaining there the hearts of men,
Who had no more its charm withstood
Than I the fragrant sandal-wood.

And ever as she moved her wrist
(A censer, scattering sandal-balm)
I saw far shores by warm waves kissed,
And sculptured profiles of the palm,
And in my heart forebodings came,
A chill — a hope — a doubt — a flame —
While drooped a rose's flowering hood
Under the pungent sandal-wood.

I FEAR NO POWER A WOMAN WIELDS.

I FEAR no power a woman wields
While I can have the woods and fields,
With comradeship alone of gun
Gray marsh-wastes and the burning sun.

For aye the heart's most poignant pain
Will wear away 'neath hail and rain,
And rush of winds through branches bare
With something still to do and dare.

The lonely watch beside the shore
The wild-fowl's cry, the sweep of oar,
And paths of virgin sky to scan
Untrod, and so uncursed by man.

Gramercy, for thy haunting face,
Thy charm of voice and lissome grace,
I fear no power a woman wields
While I can have the woods and fields.

198

IN ABSENCE.

GOD's life, but I have missed you ; in my sleep
My dreamless sleep, stone-silent and profound,
I think I must have stretched my hands to you
Because my waking hours do glean so much
Here, there, and everywhere that tells of you.

They say that 'twixt a man and woman lives
No friendship such as that of man for man.
" They say " — who says ? the lying multitude,
False prophets these, the followers of " they
    say "
And worthy not your credence, No ! nor that
Of any man's or woman's since the flood.

I call you comrade in my thoughts of you
Though you a woman be and I a man,
Since by the test of true companionship
You are as meet to be my friend sincere,
As woman is to woman, man to man ;
Have we said aught of love, unless to scoff
At arch Dan Cupid, that unlucky boy
Who hides his bow and arrows when we pass ?
Nay ! faith, for us we 'll have no more of love
Saving the love of steadfast comradeship.

A rose began our friendship ; may a rose
Its emblem be, omitting not the thorn ;
Green leaf, our hope — and in the deepening
    glow
Of ruddy petals be its fervor based,
While for the thorns, let such the record be
Of all my imperfection and default ;
And if in time the trust that now endures
Be scattered to the seven winds that blow,
The life die out, as petals fade and die —
Even in that, our friendship is the rose.

I sometimes liken you unto a rose
A yellow rose, to suit your matchless hair,
A rose to match your sweetness and your
    thorns.

II.

If you were here to walk with me to-night
The rock-built terrace where the sands below
Dip and re-dip their curves within the waves —
If you were here to name with me the stars
Or catch a glimpse of some illusive spar
Limning its blackness on the silver moon —
I had been happy, or at least content,
And reckoned not of time as one who sees
Unwilling days on drowsy wing float past ;

But you are gone, and this untiring town
That walks its bounds as tigers do a cage
Is dull indeed, for that you are away.

You say my friendship is but for a day,
I 'll grant you that an you will name to-day,
I 'll call no imprecations on my head
With jargon of the sun and moon and skies —
As warrant of my own fidelity,
But simply say, " To-day I am your friend
To-morrow, maybe not, and yesterday —
Lies buried in the sunless crypt of time."

Just for a day my faithfulness shall last,
That day, to-day, and none more loyal friend
Shall dream of you, nor wish for your return ;
And if to-morrow brings a change to us,
Some blighting of the rose of which I spoke —
Some winter chill across the flowers of June —
Think of me only as a man who kept
From sun till sun his promises to you.

Give me my dues ; that much, I 'll take no less
For resolute am I to have mine own,
And if I fail, I fail you, what of that ?
And if you fail, you fail me, that is all ;
There is no more, regret is folly's garb
An act once done, the fact alone remains.

Yet here upon the mantel of my room
Your picture waits, and what with sudden
    rain
Against the window, and my loneliness —
Approaching night, and something undefined,
I seem as restless as the restless wind ;
And some strange power doth impel me now
To rise from irksome chair and unread book,
And say, as one who speaks with heart at lip
" I am an hungered for your face again."

POPPIES.

Oh, blood-red torches of the slumbrous glow
  Light thou my steps to Lethe's dreamy main;
And daze my senses that I may not know
  The old dull throb of longing and of pain;
Grant me a respite from the light of day
  From suns that shine and pallid rains that
    weep,
Touch but my arm and lead me far away
  And seal my eyelids with a kiss of sleep.

Oh ! subtle, flowery magic ; in my stress
  Of direst need, I call alone on thee,
Since slumber's still, maternal tenderness
  More than all else is merciful to me ;
Send thou thy angels of the mournful eyes
  With rustling wings that through the dark-
    ness sweep
To streak with dusk the erstwhile reddening
    skies,
  That I may find oblivion in sleep.

Bring down the draught that to my trembling
    lips
  Sends peace and rest, while all the outer
    world
Is steeped and shadowed in a wide eclipse
  Where night's black banners are on high
    unfurled ;
Bring woven paces and the waving hands ;
  And blot the stars from Heaven's cloudy
    steep ;
From out the mystic glass let fall the sands
  And since I cannot die, then let me sleep.

I AM THY KNIGHT.

I AM thy knight, and thou hast sent me forth
To battle with the demon of despair,
To conquer self, and from its ashes bring
The phœnix of my boyhood's fervid dreams ;
To live the long, long years and make my life
Like to the sower as he passes by
Scattering the grain on rock and fertile field
To reap or lose as fate shall will it so.

No favor hast thou sent, as those of old
Wore lovingly and closely on their hearts
When they went forth to far-off Palestine,
But simply for thy word that it is best,
And for the trust and message sent by thee,
Do I go on to conquer in the fight
Of man the brute against the man divine.

Count me no idle dreamer — most of all
I pray you not on some high pedestal
Entrench my nature ; I am but a man
Who loves and hates, is merry and is sad,

Has known of gladness and has tasted woe,
And holds no higher honor to himself
Than truest love to all things true and good
And pity infinite for suffering.

Here is my hand — and to the world my scorn ;
For as I journey onward in my quest
I shall not falter, even where I fail ;
But having from the strength of thy rare soul
Caught some reflection of a light divine,
Full-armed am I, and resolute as death
To face the utmost rigor of my fate ;
To cleave to hope, to hope for happiness
To be my better self as best I can.
And so through all the lapses of gray time,
To be a man because I am thy knight.

RETROSPECTION.

THE woman tempted me, and I did fall,
From the resolve to keep my heart intact —
Sheer from the heights that cautious pride had
    reared,
Like Lucifer, from heaven down to hell,
From independence to captivity.

The woman tempted me ; by not so much
Of face and figure, as by complement*
Of all that was most sweet and womanly ;
A spirit tuned to high and pure intent,
Clear eyes which seemed when looking into
    mine,
Gray depths that harbored her unsullied
    thought ;
By not so much of figure or of face —
For who that loves shall say, " Why thus
    and so
My true love is, more fair than others are,"
Drawing her picture as a painter does,
With all the cunning patience of his art ?

Why this were simply puerile and vain
And insincere, for he whose heart is smote
By this great agony can only say,
" I love her " ; meaning she is beautiful,
Noble and true, the sum of all desire
Which makes of man a being more than
    man,
Better or worse as he himself decrees.

Somewhere in men's best efforts will be found
The saving grace of woman's influence.
And love, that in these garish later days
Is jeered at by the clay-souled common minds,
Still shines as bright, still vivifies the earth,
As Hesperus in far-off summer skies
Lights darkened paths for the blind sons of
    men.

The woman tempted me; by not a word
Nor yet a look, but as a flower might
By purity, unspotted of the world ;
For who that wanders down the thorny ways
Past sterile wastes and on through barren
    roads,
But pauses where a lone field-blossom lifts
Its dewy fragrant petals to the sun.

I cannot sigh for what is past and gone,
As clouds that flee across the flying moon,
For I am one who recks not of regret,
Save as a spur to urge to nobler deeds ;
And life is brief, I find the sunshine best
Youth and outdoors, not cloisters and old age,
And key my heart-strings to that concert pitch
Which vibrates to the happier side of things.

They say that life is solemn ; make it so ;
Go banish laughter from the swaying crowds,
Bring sackcloth, ashes, gather dead-sea fruit
And flagellate the soul with doubtfulness ;
But will you check the music of the streams
Hush the glad burst of blackbird melody
In maple branches swinging with the winds ;
Wilt blot the sunlight, hold the nimble grass
Down to the sod, or darken autumn leaves ?

The woman tempted me ; an old refrain
But most persistent, what am I to do,
Fly, fight or die, or yield as cowards will ?
My hands are tied, my very lips are sealed.
I am as one who sees a thorny rose
And in his fancy wears it on his breast
Yet in reality sees fancy fade.
This is the seed of cynicism's root,

When that a man can say, " I love," and does
    not dare
For honor's sake to break the silences
That fill the lapses of companionship.

" I dare do all that may become a man,"
So runs the precept, lighting as a lamp
The stormy seas that I must needs traverse ;
I dare do much, so honor stands untouched
Cut any Gordian knot, aye I even death's —
Rather than be a burden to my kind —
But like an Arab who has broken bread
And taken salt from out a stranger's palm
And ever afterwards remains his friend,
So I, who take her friendship and her trust
With every welcoming pressure of her hand
Dare not do more than may become a man.

Religion, creeds, the dogmas or the church,
Prayer, customs, proverbs, rules and what you
    will
And after all I hold it to be truth,
That man himself regenerates himself
Building anew the spirit's crumbling cell.

The woman tempted me ; but I have risen
Level with my temptation, stronger far

Than in that time before temptation came;
For what we meet and overcome does make
Our strength tenfold, our caution none the
    less.

The woman tempted me; I bless the day
The hour and moment, proving as they do
That I at last have something in myself
As worthy of her confidence in me.
And for the dream that lessened, for the hope
That was a dream, I happiest am in this
That time works many marvels, even I
Once grasped a fact that first was but a dream.

AT THE PLAY.

ALL the stage was alight,
And the play —
Just a comedy slight
With a touch of strained pathos dragged in by
    the way;
I remember that night
And the day that came after, a fair April day.

Yet how crude it all seemed,
Commonplace —
As the dark villain schemed
With a forced leer of hate in his imbecile face,
And you sat there and dreamed
Like a picture framed softly in ribbon and
    lace.

I had hate in my heart
Then for you,
Though I held it apart
And leaned over and smiled as most lovers
    would do,
But I knew that no art
Could teach such a woman as you to be true.

What of that, let it go ;
And again
When I think of it so,
I am cold and more cynical even than when
You whispered to know,
If I thought that most women were truer than
    men ?

And I say to you yet
'T was a play,
When we smilingly met,
And exchanged all our letters the following
    day, .
And we had no regret
That the next gusts of March did not whistle
    away.

No regret ; yet despite
All disdain ;
In the same play to-night
Where the dark villain schemes and the fond
    lovers feign,
Something blurs on my sight,
And the wraith that I see is the ghost of love
    slain.

IF.

IF, when her eyes meet mine my eyes are sealed
By the last twilight that shall ever fall,
With life and hope forever past recall
And all their longings by death's love-kiss
    healed,
Perhaps forgiveness, like some lily fair,
May bloom for him who sleeps so soundly
    there.

If, under shadows that could never cease,
I was at rest, forevermore at rest —
A knot of wildwood flowers on my breast,
If placed there by her hand might send me
    peace —
A violet cluster, taking from the skies
The summer depths of her sad, violet eyes.

If in the silence of that last long sleep,
She could but read the mystery and see,
That she alone was all life held for me,
Mayhap across her heart one pang would
    sweep,

To think that even death could make no less
The soul's dim sense of utter loneliness.

And if at last we wandering shall meet
In heavenly fields of asphodel above,
Will the remembrance of our buried love
Make the white paths of paradise less sweet —
If in the byways of that far-off land
Our journeys cross, by some lone stream, and
    we together stand?

HER ROOM.

" THIS was her room," my smiling hostess said
" And pleasant dreams ; " I thank you for the
    wish.
The clock strikes twelve, the curtains rustle
    slow
And candles on the mantel stare at me,
While light and shade, and something else un-
    seen
Blend eerily with midnight and myself.

Her room ? My room ! for did I not once
    share
These niches and these draperies with her
    thoughts ?
And doubtless she will recollect me still ;
Times change, days die, the seasons come and
    go
And many a web of winding circumstance
Will round her far-off pathway weave its
    thread,

But she remembers me, for true it is
A woman may forget all other things,
But not the memory of a man she loved.

The genius of her nature still abides
In these four walls, for I will say of her
She had the natural, artistic touch,
That makes the most of what is beautiful ;
Here is a wing of some sea-faring bird
Which curves in outward line of seeming flight,
Here is a rose — rough-sketched, but bearing
    yet
The out-door feeling in its leaf and thorn,
While higher up, an Indian arrow hangs
An emblem of the wild barbarian's art.

This is her room — and in this oaken chair
Her arms have rested many a sombre night
When the red moon sank slowly down the
    west
And Jupiter in stellar radiance
Burned like a beacon in the darkling skies ;
Here is a mirror whose quaint carven frame
Must oft have held her figure and her face ;
Oh ! happy glass to thus enfold her there
The dainty image of her dainty self,
As summer pools will hold a lily's form
In shadow.

Upon this pillow she has pressed her cheek
The pale, pale cheek, and closed her deep-
    fringed eyes,
Turned the smooth keys of Sleep's Pandora
    box
And drifted up to dim unconsciousness ;
By this wide window she has marked the
    dawn
Gild ruddily yon church's dagger-spire,
And where that grass-plat nestles by the gate
Watched morning-glories open to the sun.

What is this woman to me ?   Let me think ;
Not what she was, not as an idol now,
(The feet of clay and forehead as of brass,)
But is she part of me, a permanence,
A lasting recollection to be faced —
A joy or woe, what says the sibyl, Thought ?

And now to lend my musing wider scope
And partly for the sake of argument,
I 'll boast that I am not a common man ;
I grant my circle of environment
With its dull round of crude necessities,
But after all, my spirit looks aloft,
I am a dreamer — none the less a man.

And so when that I loved her, I contend
It came not in an ordinary sense,
But gathered all my nature in its grasp
To give her strength, and truth and tender-
    ness ;
And what she might have been was dear
    to me
A thousandfold, for men who, like myself,
Are blessed or cursed with natures like to fire,
Know in a way to duller souls denied
The keen extremes of happiness and pain.

I 'd have a woman true ; and for the rest
I 'd have her true whatever else she was,
Not aspen-like to waver in the wind,
But like to her who in the olden days
Said, wondering, " What is it to be false ? "
And I would have her strong in that rare
    strength
Which rather than it fails unflinching dares
The cord, the rack, the dungeon and the
    stake.

I 'd have the man the same — there is no love
Which from the man a lesser meed demands
Than what is asked of woman ; each to each
For their great trust should be responsible.

Where is the woman that my fancy saw !
This perfect one, did ever she exist ?
So much she had of what was credible
And if sincere, then womanly indeed ;
Why ! see, she failed in her own estimate
And failing thus, how failed she then in mine !

This is her room ; the old illusion fades
(" And pleasant dreams," my hostess' voice
    again,)
Yes, pleasant dreams, I 've worked the prob-
    lem out,
She had her goodly qualities I know,
But lacked the major chords of womanhood
And seemed all minor, being now to me
An artificial woman I once loved.

THE GRAY-EYED LADY.

SHE stood beside a lichened stone
The gray-eyed lady, all alone,
And over her the starlight shone.

And all her wealth of wondrous hair
Was black against the winding stair,
Yea ! she was something more than fair.

Upon the mystery of her dress
Above a shadow-curve's caress
Lay the wan moonshine, motionless.

Around her wrists curled shining strands
Of silver, while like welded bands,
Linked the lithe ivory of her hands.

Her face was white as are the dead,
The riddle at the last was read,
And what she said I leave unsaid.

And when she vanished from my sight
Came wraiths of days in phantom flight,
These faded, and the rest was night.

TANTALUS.

Fame? Why a fig for fame — he had marked
    its flight, a will-o-the-wisp,
When the sweet spring grass rose fresh and
    strong, and when autumn leaves grew crisp.

Gold? 'T was the basest of all base metals
    yet; better iron and steel;
And he flung his sovereigns into the dust and
    ground them under heel.

Love? And by love's deep craving alone
    (God pity him) he was curst,
As a lion that digs in the desert, and digging,
    dies of thirst.

For luminous — starlike — framed on high, a
    star that could never fall,
Was the face of the woman he loved — and
    who loved him, that was all.

ONE WOMAN.

She is a woman — subtle as her sex,
And most elusive when she seems fast bound
In reverie; I cannot make her out,
For as a flower, opening to its close
So is she changeless in unending change.
Her voice says " Nay !" her non-committal
 eyes
Veil with long lashes depths most eloquent.
And but for one rebellious dimple's crease
A smiling sign that softens else-stern lips —
I would despair where highest I had hoped
And rail at women for untruthfulness.

What is it all ? a lifted arching lid
A look distrait, an intonation clear,
A tapping of a little restless foot
Then silence and attention ; and again
A firm, sure hand-clasp that makes full amends
For what had brought me heart-ache just be-
 fore.

I love her and I love her not, for love
Such as I keep I cannot frame in words
Or at the most but brokenly, and so
I love her more in thought and less in speech,
And love her not since time is still too brief
To compass what my heart-strings sing of her ;
And what she says I say to her is true,
And what she does I do maintain is just
For might makes right and I her captive stand,
And stubborn clank my fine-spun iron chains.

She came into my life as comes at sea
To some lone shipwrecked mariner, intent,
A far gray sail that puts aside the mist
Spanning the distance with a bow of hope.

And so, and so — I love her ; grant it trite
The love of man for woman ; grant it false
In instances unnumbered — and at last
I read no peace beyond the stars on high
I find no promise in the sunlight's kiss,
And know no recompense that seems to me
As just to wait — her hand held close in mine —
Beside the one, one woman that I love.

IT'S A LONG LANE THAT HAS NO TURNING.

THE highway crosses the distant hills
Low to the west where the sun lies burning,
Sweetheart —
Though the hour is late,
And many miles before me wait,
It's a long lane that has no turning.

I study the mile-stones while I pass,
As a boy at books his lessons learning,
Sweetheart —
The end is far away,
And yet an echo seems to say,
It's a long lane that has no turning.

Your face flashed up as the sun went down,
The sweet, pale lips, and the sad eyes yearn-
ing —
Sweetheart —
I pray thee shed no tears,
For we shall meet beyond the years,
It's a long lane that has no turning.

IN THE SUNSET LANDS.

.

THE PRAIRIE.

WHERE the wild flowers, wind-shaken, their
    heads are tossing
  In this lone western land, on prairies rolling
    and vast
Here, where the whispers of solitude ever are
    crossing
  Here, if nowhere else, there is peace at last.
Rest for the heart and brain, for the soul,
    world-weary,
  In the strength and might and the beauty of
    trackless prairie.

In this far land is no taint of civilization.
  No stain of smoke — the heavens above are
    clear as glass —
With never a sign or faintest trace of any
    nation.
  Naught but a waving, boundless world of
    grass

Where over the shadows the sunshine shifts
    and lingers,
  And the weeds bend low at the touch of the
    wind's light fingers.

No voice save the voice of Nature, yet all-
    pervading ;
  Rich in its own strange music, the sweetest
    ever sung
With earth and sky and the taintless breeze
    the echoes shading,
  And all the billowy prairie overhung
With a nameless sense of loneliness and wild-
    ness,
  That thrills with its life and color the summer
    mildness.

Miles upon miles of grassy swells, sown thick
    with flowers
  In yellow and purple lines, in clusters flam-
    ing red.
Tinted with Nature's brushes and watered by
    the showers
  On the slopes, and over the hollows spread ;
On every hill their gorgeous banners showing,
  And far across the prairie in vivid colors
    glowing.

Here indeed is the keen, strong wine of free-
　　dom tasted;
　A draught once drank, it is never forgotten
　　again,
Where never a man's heart wears away, by
　　sorrow wasted,
　For Nature's moods are kinder than those
　　of men;
This is the land whose healing touch is sure
　　and painless —
　This is the land that God smiles on — the
　　prairie, pure and stainless.

AN INDIAN BOW.

THIS curved, smooth length was erst a harp
From whence the twanging echoes leaped,
Its feathered shafts with crooked grooves
In many a foeman's blood were steeped,
The buffalo-sinew stretched across
Sang sharply once in savage hands,
Resounding in the slothful wind
That drifts across the prairie-lands.

But now, like some cowed rattlesnake
All venomless, with wrenched-out fangs,
Upon the wall of this my home
The wild Comanche's weapon hangs.
The buffalo-sinew stretched across
Strikes discords in unskilful hands,
Unlike the old-time resonance
That buzzed across the prairie-lands.

A TARAHUMARI RUNNER.

Thick, rawhide sandals on his feet,
  A bronze-red figure full of grace,
Inured alike to cold and heat,
  He stands, the flower of his race :
Broad in the chest, with lower limb
  Symmetrical and hard and slim,
With breech-clout steeped in sombre dyes
  Folded securely round his thighs ;
And loosely on his massive breast
  A necklace rude of shells is hung —
By some cliff-dwelling maiden strung
  And by his coarse, black hair caressed,
His hair, from whence his dark eyes glow :
  The runner, Candelario.

Far in a savage vastness wild
  He makes his home the cliffs among,
Where chaos lies in fragments piled
  And chides the thunder's muttering tongue,

Where the red lightning's fingers reach
   All sudden through the storm-cloud's breach ;
And where the hurricane's fell wrath
   Through mountain timber sweeps its path ;
And here upon the deer's faint trail
   He follows on from day to day
From ruddy dawn to evening gray
   O'er cliff and chasm, sand and shale
Till with his knife he slays the roe :
   The runner, Candelario.

A hundred miles a day to him
   Is nothing — as with dog-trot pace
He takes departure stanch and grim,
   Nor stops nor falters in the race —
A primal athlete he, who goes
   Where the swift torrent downward flows ;
Across the steeps in level flight,
   Adown the glens and up the height —
The weary wolf will seek repose,
   And deer shall in their covert bed
Lie down and rest, while overhead
   The crow his flagging wings must close,
Yet onward speeds yon speck below :
   The runner, Candelario.

LITTLE BIG HORN.

BESIDE the lone river,
That idly lay dreaming,
Flashed sudden the gleaming
Of sabre and gun
In the light of the sun
As over the hillside the soldiers came streaming.

One peal of the bugle
In stillness unbroken
That sounded a token
Of soul-stirring strife,
Savage war to the knife,
Then silence that seemed like defiance un-
spoken.

But out of an ambush
Came warriors riding,
Swift ponies bestriding,
Shook rattles and shells,
With a discord of yells,
That fired the hearts of their comrades in
hiding.

Then fierce on the wigwams
The soldiers descended,
And madly were blended,
The red man and white,
In a hand-to-hand fight,
With the Indian village assailed and defended.

And there through the passage
Of battle-torn spaces,
From dark lurking-places,
With blood-curdling cry
And their knives held on high,
Rushed Amazon women with wild, painted
faces.

Then swung the keen sabres
And flashed the sure rifles
Their message that stifles
The shout in red throats,
While the reckless blue-coats
Laughed on mid the fray as men laugh over
trifles.

Grim cavalry troopers
Unshorn and unshaven,
And never a craven
In ambuscade caught,
How like demons they fought
Round the knoll on the prairie that marked
their last haven.

But the Sioux circled nearer
The shrill war-whoop crying,
And death-hail was flying,
Yet still they fought on
Till the last shot was gone.
And all that remained were the dead and the
    dying.

A song for their death, and
No black plumes of sorrow,
This recompense borrow,
Like heroes they died
Man to man — side by side,
We lost them to-day, we shall meet them to-
    morrow.

And on the lone river,
Has faded the seeming
Of bright armor gleaming,
But there by the shore
With the ghosts of No-more
The shades of the dead through the ages lie
    dreaming.

ARIZONA.

A THOUSAND long-horned cattle grazed
　Upon a boundless field,
And, with a shading hand upraised
　His bearded face to shield,
A swarthy herder's watchful eyes
Saw distant shadows fall and rise.

A clash of hoofs stampeded there
　Beat fast a loud tattoo,
And whizzing keenly through the air
　A feathered arrow flew ! —
A gray mustang with streaming mane
Dashed riderless across the plain.

THE SUN-DANCE OF THE SIOUX.

THE shroud of a dim, white cloud
Lifted a vapory spire,
And aloft in the sky the sun
Burned like a world on fire;
And the warriors one by one
There in the wilderness lone,
Chanted in jarring tone,
And muttered the medicine-man
As the dance of the sun began.

And high in their centre stood
A sapling of iron-wood,
And there the dancers massed
And backward and sideways passed,
While through each muscular breast
A strip of hide was strung
That taut from the upright pole
Was stretched,. as back they hung;
·And grim in the cruel test
They danced on the sterile knoll,
While chanted the medicine-man
As the blood-drops downward ran.

And back and forth they went
In the throes of that awful dance,
Now straight as a seasoned lance
And now in a crescent bent ;
While a rhythmic time they beat
With the stamp of their moccasined feet,
And out from the pole they swung
At the ends of the raw-hide reins,
While ruddy and spreading stains
From the gaping wounds were wrung.

Fierce were their sloe-black eyes
And never a brave would faint,
Resonant rose their cries
Demons in garish paint ;
And earthward the sunlight poured
As the flash of a mighty sword,
While round in a circle still
Upheld by the stoic will,
In the grasp of the raw-hide strips
With foam on their parted lips,
And their breasts pierced through and through
Leaped the warriors of the Sioux.

And the sun sank, and was gone ;
And the stars came out above
While night drew softly on
The darkness, like a glove ;

And still their shrill cries rang
Harsh and more savage grown,
As upward and out they sprang
Weird forms in the midnight shown —
Till the opaline moon had paled
And the light of the stars had failed.

Then rose the sun again
On that circle of tameless men
On wigwam and on chief,
On the grass and shimmering leaf,
On the cluster of watchful squaws
And the dogs with wolfish jaws,
While dull in a ceaseless drone
The voice of the medicine-man,
In its guttural undertone
Of strident echo ran.

And there at the turn of noon
With deep, despairing yell,
Headlong in sudden swoon
Three of the warriors fell ;
But the rest danced on and on
And tense in their breasts were drawn
The stiffening strips of hide,
As they circled side by side.

And there as the slow day waned
All weak from the dire test,
With the veins in each brawny chest
Of their glowing globules drained,
They sank on the beaten ground,
In their gory harness bound,
In the glare of the dying sun
Each brave with his bosom cleft,
Staggering one by one
Till one alone was left.

And he, on the trampled sod
One moment in silence stood,
Then broke from the torturing wood
And like to a demi-god
He towered above the rest
With his torn and bleeding breast,
And downward plunged the sun
And the dance of the Sioux was done.

A PRAIRIE MINUET.

Slow bobbing, bobbing to and fro
With awkward steps across the grass,
In solemn lines they come and go
And like to dancers change and pass.

Their ceiling is the deep blue sky,
The ball-room floor, the level plains ;
Their music, winds that hurry by
This minuet of sand-hill cranes.

OVERLAND.

A TREELESS stretch of grassy plains,
Blue-bordered by the summer sky ;
Where past our swaying, creaking stage,
The buffaloes go thundering by,
And antelope in scattered bands
Feed in the breezy prairie-lands.

Far down the west a speck appears,
That falls and rises, on and on,
An instant to the vision clear,
A moment more, and it is gone —
And then it dashes into sight,
Swift as an eagle's downward flight.

A ring of hoofs, a flying steed,
A shout — a face — a waving hand —
A flake of foam upon the grass
That melts — and then alone we stand.
As now a speck against the gray,
The pony-rider fades away.

NEZ PERCÉS.

Through the defile lay the tents to the north-
    ward
Past the gaunt spurs of the beetling Sierras,
Plain was the trail, but aloft in the mountains
Crouched the Nez Percés, and watched o'er
    the valley ;
Scanning the pathway with eyes that were
    eager
Shifting their rifles and waiting in patience,
Knowing that still to the south lay their quarry
Twenty grim troopers cut off from their
    comrades.

Faded a day and a night and a dawning
Lengthened the days, but the Indians waited
Chewing dried flesh of the deer to sustain
    them,
Reaching with hollowing palm for the water
Trickling from snow-covered summits un-
    trodden ;

Smiling but seldom, and then with a wrinkle
Of leathery cheeks as they thought of the
   troopers ;
Baleful black eyes that were lighted with
   vengeance
Hair like the raven's wing sweeping their
   shoulders
Cats of the mountain, crouched low in their
   hiding,
Patient as death, and as stern and relentless.

Miles to´ the south was the camp of the
   twenty,
Men of wild lives, but the hearts in their
   bosoms
When but the breath of the battle came o'er
   them
Rose up to meet it like steel to a magnet ;
Knowing no fear and familiar with danger
Skilled in the use of the sabre and rifle,
Sitting like centaurs their Indian ponies,
Soldiers, as brown as the grasses of Autumn.

Gray rose the moon o'er the towering
   mountains
Tipping each peak with a frost-work of silver,

Gray were the ashes where camp-fires smoul-
  dered
Sparkless as dust in the middle of summer,
Gray as a ghost was the stream that ran by
  them
There, as they mounted their ponies and
  started,
Gray and serene were the stars that hung over
Jewels of night undissolved in the darkness.

Threading their way to the pass through the
  uplands
Certain of peril and ready to meet it,
Silent as spectres they rode in the moonlight,
Moonlight and starlight a-shine on their
  weapons —
Till at the turn of a bend in the valley
Where the broad gate of the hills had been
  opened,
Right at the mouth of the canyon they halted.

Halted to tighten the girths on the ponies
Halted to wipe the night-dews from their
  rifles,
Stayed for one hand-clasp, one word from their
  leader,
Then light of heart they sprang into the saddle,

Spurred for the pass one by one, all defiant
Reckless and heedless of God, man or devil.

Each after each o'er the flint and the granite
Clattered the hoofs of the galloping ponies,
Nothing beside stirred the stillness around
   them
Till near the centre, all sudden and awful
There at its narrowest, hell broke the silence ;
One sheet of flame like the lightning, zig-
   zagging,
Leaped from the cliffs, and the sharp-snarling
   echoes
Blended with yells that the chosen of Hades
Might well have envied, could they have but
   listened ;
Then came the answering shouts from the
   stragglers
Posted along the huge rocks of the canyon,
High rose the shrill whoops of triumph and
   slaughter
Clear shone the moon with a cloudless re-
   splendence,
Ghastly and clear on that fated inferno,
While from the jaws of the gorge disappearing
Scattering sparks from his iron-shod pony,
Passed like a wraith into midnight translated
Silently still, only one of the twenty.

Red rose the dawn on the jagged Sierras
Sweet sang the birds, and the morning grass
    glistened
When from the south, to the tents at the
    northward
Rode the lone leader, the last of the twenty;
Limp hung his arm, and his stirrup was
    shivered,
Blood on his face and his forehead and fingers,
Slow lagged his pony, and still like a soldier
Upright and firmly he sat in the saddle,
Weakened from wounds so that speech almost
    failed him.

Swift rushed his comrades to seize him and
    aid him,
While from their lips came the cry " And the
    others ? "
Then with a gesture of infinite meaning
He of the lion-heart, telling the story,
Turned his thumb down, with the brown hand
    extended,
(Strange, was it not, that death-sign of the
    Roman —)
Smiled in their faces and whispered " Nez
    Percé."

A PRAIRIE PICTURE.

A LIGHT shines out in the dark northwest
   Like a star in a cloudy frame ;
It wavers, and then from the prairie's breast
   Springs up a sea of flame,
That full of a fierce desire,
Pours down in a tide of fire.

With strength that scorns all bond or shackle
   Free as the wind it rolls and leaps,
And the tall dry grasses roar and crackle
   As over the fire sweeps ;
And the gloomy, far-off sky
Lights up as it gallops by.

Into the air it darts and flashes
   Sending upward a blood-red glow,
And driving ahead the white-hot ashes
   As thick as drifting snow ;
And its fiery, scorching breath
Is as pitiless as death.

Far in its wake lie embers gleaming,
  Sparkling up as the night-winds blow,
And miles away is a red flood streaming
  With naught to mark its flow,
Save a scarlet fringe of light
On the curtains of the night.

.

.

RED CLOUD.

In the land of the Sioux the first grass was up-
    springing,
  And new on the tepees the fresh skins were
    lain ;
The bleak winter months had gone overland,
    bringing
  Far down in their wake, the last dashings of
    rain ;
The beaver peeped out of the valley morasses
  And slow on the timber his gnawings begun ;
The tethered-out horses were cropping the
    grasses
  And the Indian boys wandered wild in the
    sun.

Wandered wild in the sun with their bows and
    full quivers
  Over prairie lands wide in the far-away west,
By the hills and the woods and the reed-girdled
    rivers
  Where never the foot of a white man had
    pressed ;

And down by the village the squaws gathered
    fuel
Where little papooses in nakedness ran,
While prone on his blanket, with face cold and
    cruel,
    Lay silently smoking, — the medicine-man.

Ten braves were away to the land of the
    stranger
Whose homes lay afar in America's Alps,
Away on a foray of desperate danger
    For plunder and glory, for horses and scalps,
Lithe, sinewy warriors, with peril acquainted
    Thin-lipped and slow-spoken — long-haired
        — heavy-browed,
All eager for battle — beweaponed and painted,
    And the chief of the band was the sombre
        " Red Cloud."

Red Cloud ! His high cheek bones set off his
    grim forehead
    And the light in his eyes like an eagle's was
        fierce,
And merciless, too, as the crotalus horrid
    When he coils with his poison-fangs ready to
        pierce ;

A tower of strength and a deer for swift run-
    ning
  With limbs as of iron and sinuous grace,
No wolf was more tireless, no fox matched his
    cunning
  Red Cloud, the great chief of the mighty
    Sioux race.

To the land of the Blackfeet once more they
    had ridden
  Their ancient, inveterate, bloodthirsty foes ;
At night in the saddle, by day they were hidden
  Nor stirred on their quest till the silver moon
    rose ;
So noiseless they moved while they sped o'er
    the prairie
  That they seemed but as shadows where
    shadow shapes meet,
For the listening silence no echo could carry
  From the soft-muffled hoofs of the war-
    ponies fleet.

Ten braves and the chief gone for booty and
    pillage
  So mused through his smoking the medicine-
    man,

The pick of the tribe and the pride of the village
And choicest of all of the warrior clan ;
Twenty moons now had waned, yet no sign
had been given
The grasses grew longer, the trees were in .
leaf,
Twenty times through the heavens the moon-
man had driven
Where then were the warriors, where was
the chief ?

And as he sat scowling, foreboding disaster,
With wrinkled-up forehead, the medicine-
man,
Came the quick clash of hoofs, beating faster
and faster
As the roll of a drum — rat-a-plan, rat-a-
plan —
And there in their midst as his brave courser
staggered
With foam-whitened nostrils and fell like a
stone,
With the battle light still in his eyes deep and
haggard
Red Cloud, the Sioux chief, stood among
them alone.

And then, as the women began their shrill
    wailing
  For the souls of the braves to the Great
    Spirit fled,
The keen, savage protest, and all unavailing
  That marks the rude grief for barbarian
    dead,
Then down from his shoulder ten Blackfeet
    scalps throwing
  He said with a look as of Lucifer proud :
"Ten braves I took with me when spring
    grass was growing,
Ten chiefs have come back by the side of Red
    Cloud."

GERONIMO.

BESIDE that tent and under guard
In majesty alone he stands
As some chained eagle, broken-winged
With eyes that gleam like smouldering brands ;
A savage-face, streaked o'er with paint,
And coal-black hair in unkempt mane,
Thin, cruel lips, set rigidly —
A red Apache Tamerlane.

As restless as the desert winds,
Yet here he stands like carven stone,
His raven locks by breezes moved
And backward o'er his shoulders blown ;
Silent, yet watchful as he waits
Robed in his strange, barbaric guise,
While here and there go searchingly
The cat-like wanderings of his eyes.

The eagle feather on his head
Is dull with many a bloody stain,

While darkly on his lowering brow
Forever rests the mark of Cain ;
Have you but seen a tiger caged
And sullen through his barriers glare ?
Mark well his human prototype,
The fierce Apache fettered there.

INDIAN BURIAL.

A RUDE, high scaffold builded here
Where the wild prairie rolls away —
Stands desolate in twilight gray
Surmounted by a single spear ;
This is the Blackfoot chieftain's bier,
Thus rests at length his pulseless clay,
Watched by the shaded eyes of day
And skulking wolves that linger near.

And creakingly the rough poles shake
When the winds drift by grasses tall,
And sifting shreds of moonlight fall
On the carved death-mask, flake by flake ;
Dawns come and go, and sunsets break
Wave after wave o'er night's dark pall,
Nor heeds nor recks he of it all
Nay, who will speak that he may wake ?

His trusty weapons round him lain,
He sleeps upon this wind-swept bed

In blankets wrapped from foot to head
And under him his best horse slain —
And dreams, until the cry amain
Through the long silence far hath sped,
And then he wakes who now lies dead,
Else the Great Spirit calls in vain.

A MOUNTAIN TRAIL BY MOON-LIGHT.

THE moon-flood in the solitude
Streamed through the timber gray and cold,
And soft the night-wind's interlude
Came past the brook, which sinuous rolled
Down the old mountain like a snake ;
And all night long, with steadfast glow,
The stars in heaven lay awake
To watch the listless earth below.

And stealthily mid slumbrous air,
O'er sharp pine needles strewn with cones,
The dusk went tip-toe, here and there
And whispered in mysterious tones,
While sweeping through the vistas round
A soft-voiced zephyr seemed to bring,
Fine chords of crisp, uncanny sound
That almost made the silence sing.

Each tree was tranced in perfect calm
Dumb worshippers at Druid shrines,
While nature's censer scattered balm,
Fresh incense from the living pines ;
Each peak a statue stood, at rest,
Transfigured by the ghostly moon,
The wild-bird lay within his nest
And all the world was in a swoon.

Above a mass of jagged rock
That stamped a shadow on the sky,
A hemlock, smote by lightning shock,
Dead, blanched and grim, rose far on high ;
And suddenly across the spell
Where midnight in this vastness dreamed,
Like some dread echo out of hell
Deep in the woods a panther screamed.

THE NAVAJO.

Straight as a shaft of mountain ash
A copper-hued American ;
And round his loins was bound a sash
The raiment of barbaric man ;
And bright across his sunken cheeks
Were painted two broad scarlet streaks,
That heightened with their garish dyes
The midnight blackness of his eyes.

The buckskin moccasins he wore
With gaudy beads were thick inlaid,
And in his hand a wand he bore
Most curiously carved and made,
And on his wrist two bells he kept
That tinkled as he lightly stepped,
The talisman by which his spells
Lured serpents from their rocky cells.

Wide stretched the waste of desert lands
Beside him there ; a waveless shore,

Of burnished and of treeless sands
Like to some buried ocean's floor.
Where all year long the ruddy sun
A woof and warp of flame-thread spun,
And where the cactus reared its spike
And each parched season seemed alike.

And while the bells did music make,
Before him, and with neck upraised
And cold eyes fixed, a rattlesnake,
Turned in its coil as if half dazed ;
And moved the charmer to and fro
While undulated, smooth and slow,
As fast he paced with arms outspread —
The dull ophidian's flattened head.

Gray-mottled was the reptile's skin
Beneath the sun's rays glistening ;
And curved and crinkled out and in
The dusky coil's compacted ring ;
And fast and faster swept the chime
Of tinkling bells in rhythmic time,
The while the snake's keen vision dire
Lost something of its steely ire.

And then the savage stooped to take
Up from the twisting spiral fold,

The sinuous body of the snake,
When instantly its eyes so cold
Flashed lightning ; in that flash it sprang
Upon him ; from its hollow fang
Swift through his veins the venom leaped
And all his soul in death was steeped.

A SONG OF THE SUNSET LAND.

In the far-off hills of the sunset land ;
    In the land where the long grass bends and
        quivers,
Where the ghosts of night and morning stand
    By the gleams and dreams of the lonely
        rivers,
    There the brown sedge waving, stoops and
        shivers
At the water's edge in the sunset land.

Through the trackless paths of the sunset land ;
    Where the silence broods under far skies
        rounded
And the days slip by like grains of sand,
    There the song unsung and the chord un-
        sounded
    Seem like a part of the desert, bounded
By the wild gray wastes of the sunset land.

On the snow-clad peaks of the sunset land ;
　　As they rise in the clouds so near to heaven
In shadowy vastness, stern and grand ;
　　There gaunt old pines by the lightning riven,
　　Moan in the winds through their branches
　　　　driven,
On the crags and cliffs of the sunset land.

Mid the rolling plains of the sunset land,
　　Where the echoes drift on the tufted heather
In the wake of breezes sweet and bland ;
　　There the shadows go in a troop together
　　Across the haze of the fair June weather
In the grassy dells of the sunset land.

By the wand'ring streams of the sunset land,
　　Where the ripples rise mid the tall reeds
　　　　bending
And float away to an unknown strand ;
　　There the shade and the sunlight slow de-
　　　　scending
　　Fall where the voice of the waters blending
Sings of the sunset land.

www.ingramcontent.com/pod-product-compliance
Lightning Source LLC
Chambersburg PA
CBHW020349030726
47496CB00007B/2066